H.P

D0524265

WITNESS TO MURDER

Through her window, June Merrill idly watches her neighbour in the adjoining flats — only to see her being suddenly, savagely killed. Having watched murder being committed, June knows that she, as the only witness, is now in mortal danger . . . In *Message From a Stranger*, Mike Carr watches a beautiful woman across a restaurant. Just before she leaves with two strange men, she scrawls a cryptic note in lipstick on the table-cloth — which Mike must decipher to save her from danger . . .

Books by Norman Firth
in the Linford Mystery Library:

NORMAN FIRTH

WITNESS TO MURDER

Complete and Unabridged

LINFORD
Leicester

First published in Great Britain

First Linford Edition
published 2017

Copyright © 1946 by Norman Firth

A catalogue record for this book is available
from the British Library.

ISBN 978–1–4448–3418–5

Published by
F. A. Thorpe (Publishing)
Anstey, Leicestershire

Set by Words & Graphics Ltd.
Anstey, Leicestershire
Printed and bound in Great Britain by
T. J. International Ltd., Padstow, Cornwall

This book is printed on acid-free paper

Witness to Murder

1

Too Many Men in Her Life

'*Another* man!' Natalie Dewitt, leading musical comedy actress at the Round Theatre, gave a bored sigh. 'Very well, Suzanne, show him in.'

Suzanne, her maid, left the lounge, and was replaced almost at once by a squat, greasy man. Natalie nodded him to a seat, and he took it gingerly, plucking nervously at his scrubby moustache.

'Well, Gus? What is it *this* time?' she asked, continuing to apply make-up before the mirror above the mantelpiece. Her voice indicated that he couldn't possibly have anything of interest to say to her, but her green eyes watched him closely through the mirror with a look of apprehension.

Gus Barrows twirled his hat which he held between his hands and said:

'Listen, Natalie — that piece I read in

the newspapers this morning. Is it true?'

She turned round and looked for her cigarettes. Avoiding his accusing eyes, she lit one and puffed out the smoke. 'You mean about me getting engaged to Anthony Fulton? Yes, Gus, it's quite true . . . Aren't you going to congratulate me?'

Gus laid his hat aside and stood up. 'Natalie — you're not going through with it, are you? *You can't!*'

'Why not?'

Gus rubbed his scrubby head. 'Well, I mean to say — Fulton isn't one of your class. You'd never hit it off. He's regular society. Big noise. Important people. Don't make a fool of yourself, Natalie. You belong to different worlds.'

Impulsively he grasped her by the shoulders and stared into her eyes. She knocked away his hand roughly. She was angry now. She snapped:

'Are you trying to say *I'm not good enough* for him? Is that it, Gus? Well, I like your darned nerve . . . '

'I didn't mean it that way, Natalie. I'm thinking of what *his people* will say when they find out about your past, and that when I picked you up and gave you your chance in a show, you were just a waitress in a cheap hash-house. Can't you see what it means? How will you ever rub along with them after that?'

'They needn't find anything out,' she told him quietly, 'unless — unless *you* tell them.' A hint of danger came into her tone. 'And you wouldn't, my dear, would you?'

Gus stuck out his jaw. 'Now look here, Nat, why don't you think of someone else for a change? How about me? What do I get for the trouble I've taken with you? What do I get for making a big star out of a cheap hash-slinger? You can't walk out on me just like that. Heaven knows, I've never been demanding. I've never expected anything from you as most men would have done. You know darned well I'm crazy about you . . . always thought we might get hitched up some day.'

The woman moved her slender fingers down the clinging stuff of her dress.

She said: 'You take too much for granted, Gus. I never gave you any reason to think I would marry you, did I?'

'You know you did. You had me on a piece of string . . . Oh, what's the use . . . ? Anyway, you *might* think of the show!'

Her temper went altogether. '*Look here*, Gus, you *and* your show can go to blazes! I admit you found me as near the gutter as anyone can get, and I admit you made a star of me, and now all London flocks to see me. That's wonderful, and for what you've done, I owe you something. But remember this: until you put me in your show, you thought you would have to close down. I was hailed as a bright new personality — in other words, a fresh and more shapely pair of legs. Crowds packed your theatre, and instead of folding up, your show's still running after eight months. You owe all that to me, Gus, and I think it more than repays what I owe you. Now, get out of here. I'm sick and tired of hearing your whining!'

His face was a dull, angry red. He said quietly: 'So you're letting me down?'

'I don't call it that. But if you like to

think of it that way, yes I am. I can tell you this much, Gus: Tony — Mr. Fulton, to you — has a fortune which adds up to five hundred thousand. Five hundred thousand is just about the figure I've set my heart on getting, and now it's in my hands, I don't intend to let go easily. Whether I love him or not doesn't matter. He's young and handsome — the season's richest fish — and I've landed him.'

'Suppose I let him know exactly what kind of a woman you are,' Gus said quietly.

Her hand cracked flat across his cheek, leaving a white patch in the angry red. 'You wouldn't *dare*!'

'Wouldn't I? I wouldn't be so sure if I were you, Natalie. Do you think he'd still want to marry you if he heard about Archer? I've got proof — *hotel bills*.'

Her face was livid with rage. She rounded on him. 'Get *out*, Gus — get out before I start screaming.'

He waddled out of the room. Suzanne, the maid, who had been listening wide-eyed at the keyhole, let him out of the apartment. As he made for the lift, the doors opened, and a good-looking young man stepped out. The two looked at each other with raised eyebrows. Then Gus said: 'Er — hello, Tom.'

'Hello, Gus. Is Natalie at home?'

'Yeah — but she's not in one of her hospitable moods tonight.'

The other man grinned. 'I'll chance it . . . See you at the theatre, Gus.'

Gus nodded and entered the lift as the orchestra leader, looking suddenly tough, rang the bell to Natalie's flat. The maid said: 'I'm sorry, Mr. Archer; Miss Dewitt isn't at home.'

'Don't give me that,' he growled. He pushed the maid aside, walked into the lounge, and slammed the door. Natalie was putting on her stockings. She regarded him with irritation.

'I might have known you'd force your way in,' she said. 'Well, what is it?'

Tom Archer crossed towards her furiously and snapped: 'Look at this. Go on — read it.'

She covered her mouth with a bejewelled hand, yawned and said: 'I have read it, darling. Announcement of the engagement between Anthony Fulton and Natalie Dewitt, leading lady from Gustave Barrow's production, 'Golden Gate'. The photographs aren't very flattering, are they?'

'It's true, then?'

'But, of course, darling.'

He stared at her, his face dark and murderous. 'You devil! I ought to kill you.'

'Why? Are you afraid Tony might make me unhappy?'

'Not with his money. But how about me?'

'Oh, please, not that, darling. I've just had the same tune from Gus. What makes you men think that, simply because a woman shows a little casual interest in you, you own her body and soul? Frankly, I'm getting tired of men barging in here and throwing their weight about. I want you to get one thing clear in your mind, Tom. You haven't any hold on me. I'm a free agent, to go and do as I please. Who I marry is none of your business.'

For a moment he fought his anger, then he sat beside her and reached for her hand. She tried to snatch it away, but he held it firmly.

'Natalie, why fool yourself? You know how much I love you — and you loved me a little, too. You still do.'

She was silent, staring into space. Then she wrenched her hand free and walked towards the mirror. She turned towards him and said softly:

'Don't make it harder, Tom. Yes, I do love you, and I might have married you if I'd been the easily satisfied sort. But what could you give me? You don't make a great deal — ten pounds a week. That isn't enough for me, Tom. I earn five times that myself. Fulton can give me all I've ever wanted, everything I've ever dreamed of having. I'd be a fool not to dig now I've found gold.'

She paced the room, and then suddenly stopped in front of him. Her slim, panther-like figure was tense, but behind the beautiful, painted mask of her face Tom Archer could see the hardships which she had undergone. She looked almost like a bewildered child at this moment, with her lower lip trembling. One could almost understand how the humiliations of her struggles had given her such an exaggerated idea about money. Life had made her value it above love. There was a break in her voice as she said:

'You don't know what it's like to wonder where your next meal's coming from — to work as a waitress in a cheap café where the men maul you, and think a shilling dinner entitles them to the use of the cruet and waitress as well. You don't know that. But I do. I'm afraid of it happening again. I'm afraid of poverty, Tom. That's why I can't risk marrying you. There's no telling where we'd end up — probably in cheap theatrical digs in some dreary, provincial town.'

Tom looked at her steadily.

'Listen, Natalie, with all your money there's one thing you won't be able to buy — and it's something a full-blooded woman of your sort can't do without — '

She broke into a ripple of laughter. 'What's that?'

He walked over to her and took her in his strong arms.

'Just this — the oldest joy in the world, and the best.'

His lips pressed hard against hers. Her slim, supple body was strained to him until he could feel the quick intake of her breath.

She didn't struggle against him, and when she finally disengaged herself, her eyes were suspiciously bright.

She turned away and said: 'It wasn't fair of you to do that, Tom.'

'Natalie, my darling, won't you please — ?'

'It isn't any use, Tom.'

'You mean you're going through with it?'

'Just that. I've made my mind up nothing will stop me . . . Goodbye, Tom.'

When he had gone she suddenly felt quite alone in the world. When she turned from the mirror, there were two large tears coursing down her cheeks blurring her mascara. She said: 'Oh, damn!' Grabbing a cushion, she flung it savagely across the room.

Suzanne came in. She looked troubled

as she said shyly: 'Excuse me for talking to you like this, but do you think you're doing the wisest thing, madam? Mr. Archer is such a nice gentleman.'

Natalie shrugged, wiping away the tears from her eyes with the corner of her small handkerchief. 'I have a choice, Suzanne. I can marry for love or money. You know the kind of thing. Shall I be a rich man's darling, or shall I be a poor man's slave? I've been a slave, Suzanne, and I don't like it. I'm choosing money. Wouldn't you do the same?'

'No, madam. I wouldn't. Oh, madam, couldn't you wait a little while? It isn't wise to rush into these things.'

'Wait? Good heavens, Suzanne, no. I might wait too long. Can't you see these little lines round my eyes, the way my forehead wrinkles when I frown? I daren't wait. I'm getting old, Suzanne. I'm nearly thirty-six. And that's very old, isn't it?'

'I suppose it is, madam . . . Will you be receiving any more callers?'

'Not tonight, Suzanne.'

Suzanne went back into the sitting-room.

Natalie couldn't see through a solid oak door, otherwise she would have seen Suzanne, her young maid, staring at the other side of that door with a terrible hate in her eyes, her tiny fists clenched. She wouldn't have believed it if she'd seen it; Suzanne wasn't the type to have feelings of any kind. She was a typical lady's maid: trim, petite; and, beneath her trimness, darkly exotic. But she carefully suppressed the exotic side of her nature when on duty. Passion did not become a lady's maid, she knew. That emotion should belong exclusively to the mistress.

There was a photograph, cabinet-size, on top of the piano. Suzanne picked it up, and looked at it for a long time. Then she gave a muffled sob, and pressed it against her starched apron. Mr. Fulton didn't know — he would never know . . . but if she could help him, she would!

The maid took a sheet of notepaper from the desk, sat down and began to write. Her pen flew across the page, and the letter was quickly finished. Then she searched the desk and found a number of letters addressed to Natalie. She put three of them in the envelope with her letter, addressed and sealed the envelope, and went in search of Harry, the young janitor of the flats. He said he would deliver the letter for a kiss. Suzanne sniffed and said: 'Put it through the letter box and come away quickly. The address is 498, Levison Drive — the home of Mr. Anthony Fulton. And don't be so fresh, my lad. You're not the *only one* who's asking for trouble!'

2

To the Highest Bidder

Natalie Dewitt stood in the wings at the side of the stage at the Round Theatre, and gazed pensively at the comedian who was near the limelights, getting the silent 'bird'. Many people in the audience had come to see Natalie's exquisite adaptation of the Dance of the Dying Swan, and were impatient.

There was something uncanny in the way Natalie had captivated the public. She herself admitted that she had been lucky. Some of her steps and postures might not have satisfied a dancing mistress, but they pleased the average man.

Her gaze followed the comedian as he went into an eccentric dance, but she did not see him. Dark images haunted her . . . Gus, and Archer, whom she was letting down . . . Tony and his fortune.

Was she doing the right thing? Would she regret her greed in the years to come?

The comedian took his bow to a burst of half-hearted applause, scarcely having raised a smile. He came off, panting.

'Tough audience, Natalie,' he said. 'Can't get 'em warmed up. Maybe my stuff isn't blue enough for them. Got better hands when I worked the provinces; I had 'em rocking in *Workers' Playtime*.'

'Did you, Tommy?'

The good-natured comedian looked at her more closely, and asked anxiously:

'Are you all right, kid?'

'Yes, of course,' she replied, pulling herself together. She noticed that the stage was in a 'blackout' and she could see the diaphanous white dresses of the chorus who provided the background to the first part of her dance. The stage manager called 'Curtain!' then she was out on the boards in the wide, white circle of the limelights.

She always found the lights oppressively hot; tonight they were even more so. She went through the routine of her dance mechanically, her thoughts busy elsewhere. The soft strains of the orchestra drifted up to her, bringing her eyes down to focus on Tom Archer. He was conducting as usual; his eyes looked straight into hers reproachfully, and, for a second, she felt oddly giddy. Then she recovered and pirouetted gracefully towards the backcloth of purple.

The girls had gone now, and she was alone, going through the ritual which was supposed to represent the death of the swan. Her limbs moved more slowly. She gave a final twirl and began to sink to the stage, an unforgettable figure of grace and beauty.

Then dizziness overwhelmed her. She paused in the middle of a pivot before she crashed helplessly to the boards.

The stage manager was at his best in emergencies. Within a few seconds the curtain was down, and the stage blocked off from the audience. Minutes passed while the crowd buzzed with anticipation. Then the manager appeared on the stage.

'Please don't be alarmed, ladies and

gentlemen. Miss Dewitt has unfortunately fainted. It's nothing serious. The show will go on in a moment, and meanwhile, if there is a doctor present, we should be glad of his services. Thank you.'

A tall, fair-haired young man stood up in the orchestra stalls. He now began to push his way towards the pass door which led to the stage itself.

The manager admitted him and said: 'Miss Dewitt appears to have fainted — seems rather a bad faint, too.'

'We'll fix her up,' the fair young man said confidently. 'Lucky I happened to be here. I'm her doctor. Dr. John Brown.'

'She's in her dressing-room, Dr. Brown,' the manager told him, leading him round a pile of stacked-up pieces of scenery. They went offstage, down a red-and-cream-painted corridor, and stopped at the first door. Natalie Dewitt was still unconscious. Her features were pale and strained; she was lying on a couple of theatrical baskets with a bundle of stage clothes under her.

Dr. Brown examined her briefly. 'She'll come round in a minute,' he said.

'Perhaps you'd get me some water.'

Seconds passed before Natalie's eyelids fluttered open. She stared round and saw the young doctor. 'John! How did you get here?'

'I just happened to be in front,' he told her. 'I thought you looked a bit under the weather when you came on. What's wrong, Natalie?'

She bit her lip and looked away. Finally, she said: 'John, I'm in the most awful muddle. I don't know where I am. You — you read about my being engaged, didn't you?'

'Yes, I certainly did. You made the headlines. Not every actress has a chance to marry a millionaire in these hard times.'

'Yes, he is a millionaire,' she sighed. 'That's why I'm so worried. You see, I don't know whether I want him now. Tom Archer, the band leader, told me a lot of home truths . . . It's difficult to explain.'

'I think I know what you're driving at,' the young doctor said. 'You don't know whether to marry for love or money.' He slipped his thermometer back into its case. 'Well, don't worry. In the end you'll marry Fulton. I know you. Love doesn't count with you, Natalie. You want too many possessions.'

She sighed. 'Yes, I suppose you're right.'

When Dr. Brown had gone, her doubts began creeping back. She thought of that Sunday in the rehearsal room when she had met Tom, and of his irritation because she hadn't brought her band parts . . . That first walk together . . . The week they had played in Glasgow, and the wait for train call on Sunday mornings . . . Crewe and the refreshment buffet with its stale sandwiches under glass . . . stewed tea, and cigarette smoke. Those foolish things!

There was a knock at the door. Suzanne answered it.

'There's a young woman wanting to see Miss Dewitt at the stage door,' said the stage doorkeeper. 'Insists on seeing her.'

'Who is she?' called Natalie.

'Says her name's Fairbarn. Miss Cicely Fairbarn. She seems out for someone's blood, miss.'

Natalie calmly tapped her lips with her comb. 'Fairbarn? Why, of course. I met her at a party at Tony's place once. I'll see her, Sandy.'

Cicely Fairbarn was tall, slim, gold of hair and blue-eyed. She was dressed in the latest Mayfair creation and wore orchids high on her left shoulder. She looked utterly chic, and Natalie hated her on sight.

'Miss Dewitt,' this lovely creature said as Natalie rose to greet her, 'I expect you think I've come here with a message from Tony?'

'I thought that might have been the reason for your visit. How is dear Tony?'

'Quite dazed!' said Miss Fairbarn tersely. 'Now look here, Miss Dewitt, I don't intend to beat about the bush, so I'll say what I have to say without any preliminary sparring. You and Tony are to be married, aren't you?'

'That's the general idea,' Natalie told her coldly. 'Do you mind awfully?'

'I do, most emphatically. I'll put my cards on the table . . . '

'That's good of you.'

'Then you'll know exactly why I'm here. I love Tony, and until you came along, everything was running smoothly. I knew he was fascinated by you, but I told myself it was just a temporary infatuation.'

'Well?'

'Let me put it to you squarely, Miss Dewitt. I need Tony, and I'm swallowing my pride in coming to you and saying this — but, Miss Dewitt, I feel sure you're marrying Tony for money. His parents object to the wedding, and I've talked with them. They always thought he'd marry me, and if you give him up, he still will marry me eventually. That's why his parents are willing to pay you ten thousand pounds to step out of his life, and that's why I myself am willing to pay you an additional five thousand.'

Cecily had flustered slightly while making the offer, and now she stood tensely, waiting for Natalie to speak.

'My dear,' laughed Natalie. 'Fifteen thousand pounds to save the poor dear boy from my wicked clutches! Really! You certainly must count me a bad match for him. I wonder what he'd say if I told him that you tried to buy me off.'

'Then you refuse to accept?'

'I most certainly do. Possibly you and his precious relatives have overlooked the fact that I may love him. But in any event, I've absolutely no intention of releasing him. In fact, I'm more determined than ever to marry Tony now.'

Anger flared in the other woman's eyes. She said: 'Very well. But you'll soon regret it. I'll see to that!'

'I wouldn't make threats if I were you,' Natalie said quietly, and with a triumphant smile watched the furious socialite leave.

Somehow, Natalie was fated to build up trouble for herself — trouble and . . . *murder!*

3

Sometimes Gold-Diggers Meet Violence

While Natalie Dewitt was nearing the greatest crisis of her life, June Merrill, clad in nightgown in a neighbouring apartment, was hammering the last few words on the typewriter keyboard. She unrolled the sheet of paper, and began to check it. Then she slipped on a robe and stared out of the window, resting her hands on the ledge, and looking at the row of lighted windows in the opposite flat. There was that dancer, directly facing her — Natalie Dewitt.

Just like an actress — thinking of her 'dear public' all the time, June thought. Without drawing the curtains Natalie was preparing for bed, shedding her clothes automatically and occasionally passing a white hand across her brow. June stared curiously. She wasn't a newspaper-woman for nothing.

It seemed the actress was worried about something. June saw her pick up a cabinet-sized photograph from her dressing table and look at it. Then she tore it across savagely and threw it into the fire which was lit.

Well, well! Looks as though there's a front-page story hatching, thought June. *Headline: 'Actress Holds up Mayfair Traffic While She Spring-Cleans in Negligee.'* June peered closer. *So I'm not the only one who likes to work unfettered by too many clothes . . .*

Now Miss Dewitt was getting into bed, a pile of letters by her side on the table. Settled, she began to look through these, reading some pages, skipping others.

She stiffened suddenly, and June saw her mouth open as if she were speaking. Her gaze was fixed on a part of the room which June was unable to see, and June guessed someone must have entered.

Suddenly Natalie cowered back in the bed, her face showing horror. Then she shook her head violently in a negative gesture.

June saw a man come into the square

of room facing the window. June did not know him, but she saw him plainly. She gave a shocked exclamation as she saw the thing in his hand . . .

The man seemed to be arguing with the woman, who repeatedly shook her head and shrank away from him. Now he moved closer, his face a mask of sadistic hate. He was demanding something — something to which the woman would not agree.

Natalie Dewitt's lips opened to frame a shout for help. Then the monster pounced.

It was all over in a few seconds — right there in front of June's horrified eyes. The thing the man held — to June it seemed like a doctor's scalpel — was raised in the air. Then it slashed down viciously.

When the man moved away, the woman was squirming on the bed, and the sheets were rapidly becoming a red mass of blood from the ugly, gaping wound across her throat.

The man, turning to leave, suddenly saw June staring across at him from the opposite apartment window. He stood transfixed. June, too, was unable to move. Stunned by the sheer horror of it all, she stood paralysed, her eyes fixed on the murderer's face. It was like a ghastly nightmare from which she could not drag herself. The man broke from his own trance first. With a glare of blood-chilling ferocity, he turned, and was gone from her sight. She could read his thoughts — knew he was coming to kill her because she had witnessed the atrocity and would be able to identify him as the murderer.

Her legs still refused to obey the orders of her horror-stricken brain.

She raced panting to the door and flung it open. The murderer had come up the stairs. He was standing at the far end of the passage, peering at the doors, wondering which was her apartment. June halted with a gasp of fear. He had seen her. His eyes gleamed red and his right hand crept into his pocket. His hat was tilted at a sinister angle. He began to move.

June glanced round, hunted. The lift! It lay down a short flight of stairs. If she could reach it, get inside, dodge him, she'd be safe. She raced along towards it; and now he, too, started to run. She tried to scream, but only a sobbing gasp left her lips.

The lift gate was closed. It was automatic, and she pressed frantically at the up-button for her floor. When it purred to a halt, he was only a few feet away from her. Wildly she wrenched open the gate, threw herself inside, slammed the gate shut, and pressed the down-button fiercely. The lift started to move. The maniac would not be able to bring the cage back to his floor until she had alighted. His enraged features vanished above her as she shot down.

She could escape now! It would take him some time to get down by way of the stairs. She would have a start of a minute or two.

The lower passage was silent and empty. The janitor was asleep behind his desk at the back of the building. The front door stood invitingly open. June didn't pause a moment. She could have enlisted the janitor's aid, but old Joe wouldn't be much help. The killer would probably murder them both.

So, ignoring the aged janitor, she dashed out into the cool night, raced madly along the garden until she came to the gates, and rushed along the road towards the main street which lay about twenty yards away, unmindful of her scanty clothes. Outside the next block of flats she noticed a car, and wondered if it could belong to the murderer. It was unattended, and the motor was purring as if it was ready for instant use. She flew past it, glancing back.

A dark figure was just leaving the gate to the building which her flat was in. He glimpsed her far down the road, and made a run for the car. She didn't pause. Forcing every ounce of speed from her legs, she reached the main road. Behind her the car had roared into life.

Now amid a throng of people on the pavement, she still ran as if her life hung in the balance. They stared incredulously at the girl who was running down a London street half-undressed. But she paid no attention to them.

Her frantic eyes searched the road for a policeman — and saw one. He was standing across the road near a police kiosk, telephoning. She gasped with relief and, foolishly ignoring the steady stream of traffic, tore into the road towards him. Then blackness came over her as she pitched forward.

Brakes squealed, people shouted . . .

The policeman crossed over, holding up the flow of cars with a majestic hand. He gazed down at the body of the young girl who lay in the middle of the tarmac: a huddled, half-clad figure. The driver of the car which had knocked her down was kneeling beside her, feeling her pulse and making a rapid examination.

'It wasn't his fault, Constable,' piped an old man who had joined the throng of ghouls who always crowd round street accidents. 'She didn't give him a chance. Look how she's dressed. Must be crazy.'

'That's right,' agreed someone else. 'She just dashed out into the roadway without looking. Wonder what she was rushing about like that for in her nightgown.'

31

'Come on now,' said the constable, imperiously waving a hand. 'Let the girl get some air.'

The crowd moved away, and the driver picked up the girl and carried her towards the pavement. The constable, who was unusually bright, said: 'Well, Doctor? She all right? Don't seem to be hurt bad, does she?'

The other glanced up quizzically and replied: 'She isn't. She had a nasty bump on the head, but apart from that there's nothing more, save a slight graze on the side of the left leg. She'll be all right.'

'Had I better 'phone for an ambulance, Doctor?'

'No, that won't be necessary. By the way, how did you know my profession?'

'Couldn't miss it,' grinned the constable, proudly. 'You got a 'Doctor' sign stuck on your front windscreen. But about this ambulance, sir — if I don't 'phone, I'm liable to get into trouble if anything goes wrong.'

'Don't worry, Constable. I'll take the young lady home with me. I feel that as the accident has been my fault I ought to attend to her. I take full responsibility.'

'Very well, sir, if you say so. But it don't seem quite right to me, though, the girl being dressed as she is — '

'It's quite all right, I tell you. Here are some papers to prove who I am. The name's John Brown. My surgery is just a few minutes from here. If I give you my business card and my personal card, you'll know where to find me.'

The constable nodded and said: 'I shall have to take down particulars and get two or three witnesses in case the young lady wants to make a court case out of it when she comes round. You're sure she isn't hurt bad, sir?'

'I'll stake my reputation on it, Constable. Look, she's coming round now.'

While they had been talking, the girl's eyes had been flickering. Now she opened them and gazed blankly about her, first at the doctor, then at the policeman. John Brown said gently: 'You're quite all right, my dear. Just relax for a few minutes.'

'I'll have to take her name and address so we can tell her nearest relatives,' said the constable importantly. 'What's your name, miss? And what's the idea of running about London in your nightie?'

The girl looked at him again and frowned. Her brow knitted in an intense effort of thought. Then she shook her head helplessly. 'I — I don't seem able to — to think properly,' she faltered. 'My — my head feels awful. I — I can't remember anything. Am I really only wearing — ? How awful!'

'Help her into my car,' said the doctor; and together they got the girl into the back seat. Brown said: 'I wouldn't bother her with questions now, Constable. Shock, you know. It's a tricky thing. Suppose we leave her alone for tonight, and you send someone round to get all details in the morning or tomorrow afternoon?'

The constable scratched his head. 'Well, sir, the sergeant likes a full report immediately you know. Isn't there no means of identification on her?'

'Apparently not,' Brown told him, glancing inside the car. 'Only a Christian name embroidered on her nightgown.

J-U-N-E. June. That doesn't tell us much, does it?'

'It don't tell us nothing, sir. Must be hundreds of girls who calls themselves June.'

'Anyway, perhaps we'll get a clue from laundry marks . . . Now, I really must get her to my place, Constable. I can't answer for the consequences unless she's given a sedative soon.'

The constable nodded. The doctor's car drove away with June in the back and the crowd dispersed. As far as June was concerned, there might never have been a June Merrill because — as Dr. Brown was shortly to discover — the girl had suffered an attack of total amnesia, loss of memory. She could remember nothing of her previous life, nor could she recall the ghastly events which had led up to her being involved in the street accident.

⋆   ⋆   ⋆

'Come in,' said Dr. Brown pleasantly, opening the door for the alert-looking young man and admitting him into the

35

library. 'I expect you're from the police, aren't you?'

The plain-clothes man nodded. 'I've called about the accident which took place last night, Doctor,' he said. 'You brought the young lady to your home here, I understand.'

'That's quite true. Do you want to see her?'

'If she's well enough.'

'Perfectly. There's no physical injury apart from a bump on the head, and a grazed leg which I dressed and which is now quite comfortable. But there is one thing about which I should warn you.'

'What's that, Doctor?'

'The girl is suffering from a total loss of memory. She can recall nothing. Sometimes this does happen in cases of concussion. I must ask you not to upset her in any way, because she has had a very severe shock, and any excitement might cause a relapse. You understand?'

'I think I do, Doctor. If she can remember nothing, I don't see much point in questioning her, but the routine has to be gone through. Where is she now?'

'Upstairs in the spare room. Mrs. Higson, my housekeeper, is looking after her for the moment; and later on Miss Garner, my nurse-receptionist, will be along. Now, please don't try to force her memory, whatever you do. Amnesia victims can sustain very severe setbacks if they are confronted with their pasts too suddenly.'

The girl they knew only as June was propped up by pillows, looking a little strained, but quite healthy. As they came in, she looked towards them and frowned in a puzzled way.

The plain-clothes man took a chair by the bed.

'These are just routine questions, miss,' he said gently. 'First of all, do you remember your name?'

She shook her head.

'Doesn't the name 'June' suggest anything to you?'

'I'm afraid not.'

'H'm. Can you remember your address?'

'No, I'm sorry, but I can't. I know it's awfully stupid of me — '

'That's quite all right. We'll trace you eventually. Can you tell us how you came to be running through the streets late at night, in your nightclothes, and obviously in a tearing hurry?'

'Did — did I do that? I just can't remember anything. I wish I could — but I can't.'

'You feel quite well otherwise?'

'Quite, thanks to the doctor here,' she said, smiling at John Brown. 'I'm in very good hands.'

The plain-clothes man rose and said: 'Well, there isn't any point in asking further questions at this stage.' He picked up his hat. 'Perhaps I can call round again when she's recovered, Doctor?'

'Yes, that would be the best plan.'

When the Scotland Yard man had gone, Dr. Brown sat at his desk, and the lines of worry in his young face were more marked . . . He toyed with a paper knife nervously as he thought of the girl in the other room.

4

A Woman's Wild Past

Superintendent Weather, of New Scotland Yard, was puzzled and irritated. His irritation sprang from the facts — or lack of them — surrounding the murder of Natalie Dewitt, the actress. For the fifteenth time, he combed her flat, searching for anything which might provide a clue. He didn't even find a button.

'It's a hard world when it comes to real life,' he said, rising and dusting the knees of his trousers. 'In a novel, the detective would at least find a cigarette stub of a peculiar brand, and from that clue he would deduce that the killer was a tall man about forty years old, with a stoop and a slight limp in the right foot, and that his shirt size round the neck was fifteen! But this isn't a novel. It's real life, and the only cigarette end we found probably belongs to the girl who was murdered . . . Have you unearthed anything new, Jackson?'

Inspector Jackson started guiltily. He hadn't even been looking.

'Er — no sir, nothing fresh,' he said.

'Then bring in that maid and we'll have her questioned. We must find out who committed this crime, Jackson. The Dewitt woman knew a lot of important people, and the Home Secretary's keeping an eye on this case. Things are likely to be sticky.'

Suzanne, the maid, entered the room in response to a call from Jackson. Her eyes moved nervously to the blood-soaked bed.

'Now then, miss,' began the superintendent. 'Start from the beginning again and tell us all you know.'

Suzanne nodded nervously. 'I don't know much, sir. I had a telephone call, asking me to meet someone — '

'A man?'

She hushed and looked uncertain. Weather said: 'Now, miss, you must tell us. Remember that you're in a very serious position.'

'Very well, sir. I went to meet Anthony Fulton, Miss Dewitt's fiancé. He telephoned and asked me to call at his home.'

'That's interesting. The dead woman's fiancé, eh? Carry on, and don't hold anything back.'

'Well, I went to see him about a letter I sent him yesterday afternoon. He wanted to ask me some personal questions about — about Miss Dewitt. Madam had gone to bed, so I sneaked out to keep the appointment. I met him at his home in Levison Drive, and we stayed there talking until almost two in the morning.'

'Wasn't that rather unusual?'

'Oh, of course it was, sir. But it was important.'

'Really? What matter did you discuss until such an hour?'

Suzanne shuffled nervously, and her fingers tightened on the back of the chair. 'It was — was about Miss Dewitt's — former lovers,' she said almost inaudibly. 'I didn't want madam to take Mr. Fulton in, sir.'

'Why? What was your interest in the man?'

'I know it sounds silly, sir, but I — I was in love with him. I've seen him here often, and he was so nice and pleasant to me. I — I hated the idea of Miss Dewitt making a fool of him. She was only after his money. She often said so.'

'I see. So you went and told this man all about your mistress's past.'

'Yes, sir. I sent the letter by the janitor yesterday afternoon, and it seems Mr. Fulton didn't receive it until late because he had been out for the day. When he did get my note, and read the letters I'd sent — letters which Miss Dewitt had had from her lovers — he 'phoned me at once and asked me to come over so as we could get things straight.'

'And you left the flat immediately?'

'About ten-thirty, sir. I got back at a little after two.'

Weather nodded and said: 'Jackson, what time did the surgeon estimate the time of death?'

'Between eleven-thirty and twelve.'

'If that's correct it exonerates this

young lady,' said the superintendent weightily. He seemed more affable to the maid now. 'What happened when you returned?'

'I went straight into my room and to bed, sir. I felt a little ashamed of what I'd done. Miss Dewitt used to trust me, you see, and she was often very generous. I hadn't liked the idea of double-crossing her. I slept until my alarm went off at eight-thirty. We aren't early risers here. Then I dressed, made coffee, and went to call madam. I — I found her lying there . . . ' She broke off and covered her face with her hands. 'It was horrible . . . I called you at once — 999. They'd often said on the wireless that was the right thing to do.'

'You disturbed nothing?'

'Oh, no, sir. I was too frightened.'

'With regard to Miss Dewitt's fiancé — how did he take the accusations you made against her?'

'I — I don't know. He was talking to me for a long time — trying to see if I was lying, I think.'

'And you satisfied him you weren't?'

'I don't know. He didn't say one way or the other. But he did take notice of the letters I had sent. They were very frank letters.'

'You're sure you left at two o'clock?'

'About that time, sir. I remember saying, 'Goodness! Look how the time's flown.' It was ten to then. We chatted for a little while longer and I came straight home.'

The superintendent grunted. 'Do you know of anyone with whom Miss Dewitt may have quarrelled recently? Anyone who might wish her — dead?'

The maid shook her head. 'No. She had quarrelled with people, but not very much. I'm sure none of them would have murdered her.'

'Now, tell us what the quarrels were about, and with whom she quarrelled. No matter how slight the argument, it may have a bearing on her death. Please try to remember everything.'

Suzanne began to talk, telling them about the first quarrel with Gus Barrows, the show owner; and then of the argument with Archer; and the visit of

Cicely Fairbarn to the theatre. Weather nodded wisely, and Jackson made copious notes in his book. 'That was all, sir,' concluded Suzanne. 'I didn't actually hear the quarrel with the society girl, but madam told me about it on the way home.'

'Thank you, Suzanne. You've been very helpful. You may go now, but remember you may be needed for further questioning. I must ask you not to leave your present address.' The superintendent jerked his head towards the inspector. 'Call the janitor.'

Harry, the janitor, was a beetle-browed lout with a protruding paunch and a surly manner. He slouched into the room and drooped against the table edge, a cigarette dangling from his lips. Weather frowned and snapped:

'Take that smoke out of your mouth, man. Stand straight.'

'Wot for?' said Harry morosely. 'Who the 'eck do you fink you are — a blithering sergeant-major?'

'You're under suspicion of murder, and I'm here to question you. I advise you to answer promptly and civilly. Now, let's take your spells of duty. How do they fall?'

The janitor's expression showed that he hadn't much respect for law and order. He said in a surly tone:

'Just at present I'm on from four noon to four of a morning. Twelve hours steady. On me feet most of the time. It's murder!'

'You're darned right, it is!' snapped the superintendent. 'Now tell me — could anyone enter the flats without you seeing them?'

'Naw. Not unless they was invisible.'

'Don't try to be funny,' growled Weather. 'Think back and tell us exactly who came in and out between the hours of ten and twelve last night.'

Harry scratched his head reflectively. 'Lessee. About 'arf past ten Miss Dewitt's maid comes down and goes aht. About quarter of eleven, the doctor wot attends to Miss Dewitt comes on the scene and goes up to see her. Brown, I thinks 'is name is — Dr. Brown — well, he parked 'is car ahtside while 'e went up.'

'When did he come down again?'

'I can't rightly say. You see, at about eleven I goes dahn into the basement to 'ave me supper. I didn't get back until nigh on twelve. 'E'd gorn then; 'is car wasn't at the kerb.'

'And after that no one entered or left?'

'Not until the maid comes back at about two o'clock. I see her come in and go up.'

'So, while you were having supper, anyone might have gone up, committed the murder, and gone away again without you knowing?'

'I expects so.'

'About the dead woman — did you know her well?'

'Not too well. I knew 'er maid as well as might be. I used to go errands for 'er, see.'

'What kind of errands?'

'Nothing important. Things like fags and that, and an odd bottle of whisky for 'er lidyship.'

'You delivered a note to someone for her yesterday?'

'Yus, I did that. To a Mister Anthony Fulton, of Levison Drive. 'Is valet said 'e wasn't in, so I left it for 'im for when 'e came back.'

'Anything else you can tell us?'

'Naw.' Harry picked his teeth with a matchstick. 'You needn't think as I did it, see. I wouldn't soil me 'ands on ruddy actresses — 'specially actresses like 'er. Wot that maid of hers didn't tell me about 'er — blimey, it don't bear repeating!'

'So, you didn't approve of Miss Dewitt?'

'Me approve of 'er and 'er goings-on? Not blooming likely! I useter watch 'er feller coming up to see 'er often enough — the one called Archer — that was afore she got engaged to this Fulton feller. I remember thinking 'e deserved orl 'e got from 'er. I 'ates 'er kind — but,' he added cautiously, 'that don't mean I'd do 'er in. I'd watch it, I ain't looking for trouble.'

'Hmm. Well, whether you'd do her in or not, you're under suspicion, and I want you to hold yourself in readiness for further questioning. You can go now.'

As Harry left, a plain-clothes man walked in to the room.

Weather said: 'Any luck?'

'No, Super. I questioned everyone on all floors, and no one saw or heard anything.'

Weather crossed the room and pointed to a window opposite, saying: 'See that window over there? I'm wondering if whoever lives in that place saw anything. It's a possibility. They might have seen someone in here with the Dewitt woman. If so, they may be helpful to us. I think we'll try that angle before we start getting in touch with the other suspects. See that the girl and the janitor don't leave the building. If they've cooked anything up, I don't want them to get in touch with anyone outside until I've finished questioning Fulton, Barrow, and this Fairbarn girl. Then, of course, there's Dr. Brown. So far he seems to be our prize bet. Pity: I've always liked him.'

As they descended to the hall, the postman was slipping letters into the rack. Weather glanced at them, took down one addressed to Natalie Dewitt, thumbed it open, and read it quickly. It bore a postmark of that day's date; the

49

time of posting said eight a.m., the morning post; and, since it was local, it had been delivered with the midday delivery. Weather handed it to Jackson. It read:

My Dear Natalie,

I have had rather a shock; I am in possession of some letters — which may be forged — and some slanderous information, which I really cannot believe. I must see you as soon as possible, so that you can set my mind at ease. Of course, I think the whole thing's ridiculous, but my informant is someone who is very near to you, and if she is prattling maliciously, she should be dismissed. Meet me for dinner at the Savoy, and later we can go to Levison Drive and talk it all over.

I feel too upset to speak to you now; that is why I am sending my message by letter. Until tonight —

My Love,
ANTHONY

Weather grunted and placed the letter in

his pocket. Then the two crossed the sooty lawns to the other block of apartments. The janitor was industriously sweeping out the passage, but a few crisp words put him wise to the situation, and he escorted the two Yard men up to flat thirty-three. Weather knocked and, receiving no reply, pushed open the door.

'Queer!' he mused. 'Electric light on at midday — fire burnt out — radio going, and no one here!'

He picked up a sealed envelope from the desk, glanced at it, and laid it down again. He noticed a woman's outdoor coat and hat which lay on the settee. He turned to the janitor and said: 'Who rents this flat?'

'A Miss June Merrill, sir. She's an author.'

'The absent-minded type?'

'Not at all. She doesn't go out much. Just sits and hammers that machine all day. Can't understand why she'd leave the lights and radio on. Maybe she's in the bedroom or the bathroom.'

'Try them, Jackson,' Weather said.

While Jackson made a quick search, the

superintendent stood glancing round, noting the open book lying on the chair arm and the uncovered typewriter. The cigarette which had been laid in an ashtray had burnt itself out in a long column of white ash.

He looked from the window, and noted the position of the bed in the room across the block. He turned back thoughtfully to hear Jackson say: 'Nobody here, sir.'

'Seems we may be on to something,' Weather said. 'Jackson, get a description of this Merrill girl, and send out wanted-for-questioning circulars. Call all stations. Give the story to the papers and ask them to publish a full description of the girl. Do that now. I'll see if I can contact the night porter here.'

'He's in the building, sir,' said the day porter. 'We have rooms in the basement. I'll take you down if you like.'

'You stay here and give a description of this missing girl to Jackson, and if she returns when we've gone, be sure to let us know at once. I'll find my own way to the cellars.'

'Not cellars, sir — basement,' said the

porter, aggrievedly.

'Sorry — basement, then.'

Weather took the lift down to the bottom floor, decanting himself into a passage which was scarcely as luxurious as the rest of the place. He wandered along until he reached a door which bore the lettering: NIGHT-PORTER. He knocked and entered in answer to a squeaky, 'Come in.'

'You the night-porter here?'

'That's me,' agreed the weedy man lying on a small bed. 'Who are you?'

'Superintendent Weather, Scotland Yard,' Weather said. 'I'm trying to locate a young lady who has a flat here. The name's June Merrill — number thirty-three. Know anything?'

'Isn't she in her rooms?'

'Not a sign of her.'

'Then I can't help you at all. You'd better ask my mate who's on days if he saw her leave this morning.'

'Seems he hasn't seen her, either. You're sure you didn't see her going out last night — say about twelve or so?'

'Blessed if I could say. I was asleep then

— had been since about eleven-thirty — didn't wake up until one or two.'

'Do you usually sleep on duty?' snapped Weather.

'And why not? Nobody minds. I'm only here to keep an eye on the place. I'd wake up fast enough if anything went wrong.'

'I doubt it. Apparently something went very wrong last night, but you didn't wake up, did you?'

The porter couldn't think of an answer to that one. Weather grunted: 'All right, Rip Van Winkle. You'd better try hard to remember. We'll deal with you later.'

Jackson was waiting for him in the hall. 'Any luck, sir?'

'None. Get the description?'

'Yes. The girl's pretty good-looking from what the porter tells me. I'll send out a circular from the Yard. If she's anywhere in London, we'll find her. What now, chief?'

'Back to the Yard, and while we're having lunch, I'll have our suspects roped in for questioning. We'll send a squad car for Dr. Brown, and one man can follow it and search the vehicle he owns. If he did kill her, and had the car with him as the porter says, there might be a clue to be picked up from it. Bloodstains, hairs — things like that.'

'It looks pretty black for this Dr. Brown, doesn't it?' Jackson mused. 'D'you suppose he did it, Super?'

'How should I know? If we can find a motive, it's quite likely he did. But so far he's the only one who *hadn't* a motive. Even Harry, the janitor, had a bigger motive than his. Barrows had a good motive for wanting his own back, so did Archer and this Fairbarn girl. The maid isn't any too innocent. The trouble with this case is that we've got too many suspects and no clues. We'll just have to see what happens when we've roped 'em all in for questioning. I have a feeling it'll be rather interesting. We can eliminate one or two, perhaps, if they produce alibis — but those who don't will be in an awkward position. Very awkward. I have a feeling Dr. Brown will be one of them! Remember that Jack the Ripper was supposed to be a doctor . . . '

5

At the Mercy of a Maniac?

'Feeling better now, June?'

June looked up and nodded gratefully. Dr. Brown smiled, patted her hand and said: 'Your appetite hasn't suffered, anyway. You did justice to your lunch. But I must get along to my surgery now. I had to give it a miss this morning, and I expect my patients won't be feeling too pleased with me.'

'I'm sorry to cause you so much trouble,' June said. 'I often wonder why you take so much trouble over me.'

The young doctor looked at her closely and then smiled.

'Forget it. There isn't very much wrong with the majority of my patients anyway, believe me. Nothing that a spot of hard work won't cure — though, unfortunately, I can hardly tell them that. Most of 'em are quite convinced they're the most delicate person in Britain. I mustn't mention names, but a certain titled lady I treat is firmly convinced she suffers from some incurable ailment whereas all she really has is a touch of wind every now and then . . . '

June laughed; then she looked at the handsome doctor wonderingly. He seemed so absurdly young to be an established specialist with a large practice and many important people as his patients. Nor did he talk quite as she would have expected a distinguished young doctor to talk; he was too natural — at least with her. Perhaps he adopted a different approach with his wealthy clients.

'Any sign of the memory returning yet?' he asked her lightly as he struggled into coat and hat.

She shook her head, the old puzzlement returning to her eyes. 'Not even a glimmering. I feel an awful fool.'

He said gently: 'Don't worry about it. Relax, and give yourself a few days' complete rest. I feel sure your memory will come back before long . . . There's no hurry. You're more than welcome to stay here as long as you like. Now, don't strain. Just leave it to the police to find out who you are.'

The doorbell rang, and he crossed towards the hall. She heard his footsteps against the polished parquet and heard the subsequent conversation.

'Are you Dr. John Brown?'

'Yes, I am.'

'I'm from Scotland Yard, sir. Superintendent Weather wants to ask you some questions.'

'Questions? About the young lady who's lost her memory, I suppose?'

The C.I.D. man was guarded.

'I don't know anything about that, sir.'

There was a moment's silence; then the doctor came back and said to June: 'I seem to be wanted at the Yard. Heaven knows why! Will you ring up my office for me, please, and tell my receptionist, Miss Garner, where I've gone? She was supposed to come and look after you when I reached the office, but I'm afraid that's impossible now. Mrs. Higson will be able to get you anything you need, though, and probably they won't detain me long. I'll see you again tonight. Perhaps we might have a quiet game of cribbage together.'

During the drive to the Yard, the doctor was thoughtful and silent, not even attempting to discover why he was wanted. He was content to wait and get the facts from Weather, whom he knew slightly, having assisted in one or two cases in the past.

In the anteroom to Weather's office, some other people were assembled — three men and a woman. They all seemed quite puzzled, and the woman was twisting a tiny handkerchief between her fingers. Weather popped his head out of the office and said: 'I'll see you first, Doctor.'

Brown went in and took the chair which the superintendent indicated. Weather was in serious vein, his forehead corrugated into a permanent frown.

He began: 'First of all, Doctor, I want you to realise that you are not here to give us any professional help this time.'

'I'm not?'

'Unfortunately, no. I'm questioning you on a very grave charge, and I should warn you that anything you may say — well, you know the rest of it, don't you? As a matter of fact, silly as it sounds, you happen to be suspect number one.'

'Really?' Brown said in amazement. 'I feel flattered, Superintendent. What exactly am I suspected of?'

'Murder!'

The young doctor chuckled. 'If I didn't know you so well, I'd say you were having a little joke with me. Whom have I murdered?'

'We don't say you murdered anyone, merely that you are suspected of murdering someone.'

'Well then, whom am I suspected of murdering if you want to split hairs?'

'One of your patients, Doctor. A Miss Natalie Dewitt.'

Brown half-rose from his seat and said: 'Natalie? Good God! Murdered? She can't be, Superintendent. Why, I was talking to her only last night.'

'We know you were, and that's what places such suspicion on you. The woman was murdered round about the time you were with her, or immediately afterwards. It happened in her bedroom after she had retired. The porter of the flats claims to have seen you go up to her, but he didn't see you come down. Suppose you tell us about your visit.'

'Certainly. I knew Natalie very well. We were more like friends than doctor and patient. Last night she collapsed on the stage during her number, and I went round to her dressing room. She was greatly worried about personal matters, and asked my advice, which I refused to give.'

'Why did you adopt that attitude, Doctor?'

'The things which were troubling her weren't of a medical nature. I told her to get home and go to bed and give her mind a rest. After I had got home from the show, I decided perhaps a sedative would help her. I was pretty sure sleep wouldn't just come to her naturally. I went back to my surgery for luminal and then took the tablets to her. She seemed a bit annoyed about something. Apparently her maid had sneaked out without telling her she was going. Well, I gave Miss Dewitt two tablets, and took her temperature, which was slightly above normal. Apart from that, she was quite well when I left.'

'What time was that?'

'Let's see . . . I got there at about quarter to eleven by my dashboard clock, and I was there about twenty minutes. I must have left about five past or ten past.'

'Then you'd be home again before half-past?'

'Actually, no. I decided a short drive wouldn't hurt me, and I took one to blow away the cobwebs.'

'That means that you have no witness who could swear you left the flat before eleven-thirty, doesn't it?'

'I expect it does.' Brown tried to yawn. 'What difference does that make?'

'A great deal, Doctor. The surgeon's report puts the time of death after eleven-thirty, and a jury might think it odd for a man like yourself to be taking pleasure jaunts in your car late at night. What time did you actually arrive home?'

Brown shook his head. 'That I can't say, Superintendent. I had an accident on the way. A young girl ran out in front of my car and was knocked unconscious.'

'Then the time of that accident will be booked in the policeman's report.'

'How did you know a policeman was on the spot immediately?' said Brown.

'A policeman always is,' said Weather smugly. 'Tell me, Doctor, is the girl all right? Not injured?'

'Not physically. But her memory seems to have gone. She was wearing only a nightgown and dressing robe when I hit her. It looked as if she'd run out of somewhere suddenly, on an impulse — maybe fright. She didn't look where she was going at all. The only identification mark on her was a name embroidered on her nightgown — a Christian name — June.'

Weather had been portraying excitement during the last few sentences. Now he stood up and leaned forward. 'Where did this accident take place? Was it near Natalie Dewitt's flat?'

'As a matter of fact, it was. On the

main road nearest her flat. I'd driven in a circle and was just turning homewards.'

Weather sank back heavily into his chair. He was breathing hard. He said: 'Good grief! It must be the same girl. What does she look like, Brown?'

Brown seemed a little surprised, but gave an accurate description of the girl.

Weather turned to Jackson and said: 'Cancel those circulars giving the girl's description. We've found her. Where is she now, Doctor?'

'I took her back to my own home.'

The superintendent jerked forward. 'Why?'

Brown shrugged. 'I felt I owed it to her. After all, it was I who was responsible for her loss of memory.'

'Yes,' said Weather meaningfully. 'It definitely was you. Well, we'll send someone along to bring her here, and then we can question her.'

The young doctor said firmly: 'I don't know just what connection the girl can have with the murder, but I've already told you that questioning her won't do any good . . . Her mind is a blank. If you start moving her about, you might easily delay her recovery. Remember, Weather, I may be number-one suspect, but I'm still the young lady's medical adviser . . . '

'Self-appointed,' said Weather.

'Self-appointed, as you say, but still her adviser. I'm warning you that if you move her and try to force her to remember, you'll have to take full responsibility.'

Weather groaned. 'But it's important to you that we get at the truth, Doctor. We believe that girl knows who the murderer really is. If it isn't you, you have no reason to be afraid of her regaining her memory.'

'I don't give a damn whether she exonerates me or not,' snapped Dr. Brown, his patience dwindling. 'I'm thinking of the girl herself. You mustn't upset her with your confounded questions. It would be criminally stupid.'

Weather tugged at his scanty locks helplessly. 'I suppose you think we're going to leave her in your charge, eh? Well, suppose you did murder the Dewitt woman? Suppose you knew June's recovery would pin the killing on you? Don't you see, man, your attitude is incriminating you even more?'

Dr. Brown sighed. 'I *want* the girl to get her memory back, because then I know she'll clear me of this ridiculous suspicion. But she'll never remember if you start third-degreeing her now.'

'Look,' said Weather patiently. 'Late last night, a woman had her throat cut. You are suspected on purely circumstantial evidence. Therefore, even if I don't hold you on suspicion, I certainly can't let you be in a position where you could interfere with the girl's recovery. Sorry, Brown, but I'll have to turn her over to another doctor.'

Brown nodded and said, his eyes slightly narrowed: 'Very well. But be sure you post a man to keep an eye on her. Whoever the real murderer is, he's likely to try to get her out of the way if he thinks she may talk.'

He broke off abruptly as a detective entered excitedly. Weather said to the doctor: 'I took the liberty of sending a man along to search your home and car while you were out. Hope you don't mind, Doctor. Routine, you know.'

'Not at all,' said Brown. 'But you've got a heck of a nerve!'

The detective looked at him, then at Weather. He was bubbling over with achievement.

Weather said: 'Well? Did you search the garage and the house?'

'I didn't need to, Superintendent. I found all the evidence we need in the garage — in a side pocket of the car.'

The detective fumbled in his pocket and drew out a clean handkerchief. He unrolled it and laid it on the desk, revealing damning evidence against the young doctor.

All eyes turned accusingly to Brown, who said: 'I swear I've never seen those before in my whole life.'

But he had to admit that these exhibits, which the detective claimed to have found in his car, made things look particularly black for him. After all, when a woman's had her throat cut, and one of the suspects has a blood-stained scalpel — and an equally blood-stained glove — found in his possession, it does make things a trifle awkward!

★ ★ ★

'They all have alibis,' said Weather. 'All except Dr. Brown.'

It was much later. The suspects had been questioned, and each had supplied foolproof alibis which corroborated where they had been at the time of the murder. Gus Barrows had been playing poker with the members of the orchestra, including Tom Archer. Cicely Fairbarn had gone to bed comparatively early, and although she might have sneaked out from her home, Weather didn't think she had. Anthony Fulton and the maid had been talking together at Fulton's place. Only Dr. Brown was unable to provide an alibi.

'The way I see it,' said Jackson, 'is like this: Brown went to Miss Dewitt's flat and killed her. He was seen in the act by June Merrill. She rushed out in panic, and started running down the road, no doubt realising that Brown would have to kill her because she was the only witness. Brown got his car, followed her, saw she was getting away, and deliberately ran her down. Maybe he hoped to kill her, but didn't quite manage it. Then he took her to his own home so that, if she showed any signs of recovering her memory, he'd be able to do something about it. When he got in the car to follow her, he was in such a state of nerves, thinking he'd been spotted, that he thoughtlessly slipped the glove and the scalpel in the car pocket. Later, he forgot it.'

Weather grunted and looked wise. 'I thought that was how you'd see it. Can't see any farther than the tip of your red nose, can you? Content to take the easiest way, as usual, eh?'

Jackson looked hurt.

'Well, what else could it have been then? Do you mean to say you don't think it was Brown, sir?'

'It may have been, but there're one or two things which don't ring true.'

'Such as?'

'Such as that glove.'

Jackson scratched his head and said: 'Eh?'

'The glove, man. Look at it. Go on.

What do you see?'

'Just a glove,' said Jackson doubtfully.

Weather smiled grimly. 'I expected you would. In fact, I'm surprised you can even see that much. Doesn't anything else about it strike you as being odd?'

'No. Why should it? A glove's a glove, isn't it?'

Weather sighed wearily and said: 'All right. We'll leave that for the time being. Now take the scalpel — do you suppose it's likely that a doctor would use a thing like that to commit a murder?'

'Of course he would. It'd be natural.'

'Yes, natural if he wanted to be suspected. But wouldn't it be far more natural for whoever did the killing to use a scalpel with the intention of *throwing suspicion on* the doctor?'

Jackson shook his head helplessly. He said: 'But who else could have done it?'

'That's what we'll have to find out. Far too many clues point to Brown. That's what makes me think he had nothing to do with it at all. I see the crime this way: the killer, whoever he was, was on the spot when Brown arrived. Perhaps he'd been hanging round, awaiting his chance. When he saw Brown go up, he got the idea of throwing the blame on him. We must assume he knew where he could lay hands on a scalpel, and went to get it at once. Meanwhile, Brown left, and the killer knew he'd gone because his car was no longer outside.

'The janitor was still having his supper, and the killer went upstairs silently. He found the woman in bed, killed her, and was probably seen by the girl in the opposite flats. She ran out in panic, still wearing her nightclothes. She got herself knocked down by Brown's car as he was coming back from his fresh-air drive. Well, Brown drove her home, followed by the murderer, probably in his own car. Brown would have to leave his car in the drive while he took the girl into the house. While the car was there, the killer slipped the glove and the scalpel into the side pocket, ready for the police to find.

'That's my theory — and the person responsible was one of the people in this office this afternoon. That bloodstained glove we found was the real killer's one slip. Brown is right-handed — and that glove is a left-hand glove! All you have to do now is to find out which suspect among the people we had in the office this afternoon is left-handed; and then, my lad, you've got the murderer!'

Weather smiled with happy superiority. But his underling had grave doubts. In the past, he'd had several occasions to doubt his chief's powers of deduction.

6

Rehearsal for Horror

'That's all for now, folks,' said Jackson, pushing his head into the anteroom. 'You people can go; all except you, Doctor.'

'You mean we aren't wanted any more, eh?' asked Anthony Fulton. 'It's about time, too! If you must drag perfectly innocent people into a mess like this, you might at least provide a comfortable waiting room for them.'

Jackson looked at the tall young man and said: 'We may need you again, sir. Don't leave town.'

'We're still under suspicion; is that what you mean?' Fulton asked. 'Don't worry, Mr. Jackson. I haven't anything to fear from you people. I'll still be around when you want me.'

He linked his arm through that of Cicely Fairbarn's and made for the office door. Then he turned and said over his shoulder, 'Are you arresting anybody, by the way?'

'Well, sir,' said Jackson, 'since the lady was engaged to you, I suppose there's no harm in you knowing. The superintendent is holding Dr. Brown on a charge of murder.'

Tom Archer glared malevolently at the doctor and snapped: 'By heavens, if I could be sure you did kill her, Brown, I'd — I'd strangle you with my bare hands.'

'Take it easy, Archer,' growled the doctor. 'You're almost as big a fool as the police.'

Gus Barrows contented himself with looking sympathetic. Leaving the others to go, Brown accompanied the inspector into the inner office.

'Is that right, Super?' he asked, settling in a chair again.

'About holding you? Do you think it was a bluff? What would you say if I said I *am* going to hold you, Doctor?'

Brown forced himself to be calm. 'I'd say you hadn't any option. But I'd also tell you what a mistake you'd be making. Well, in view of the evidence, there isn't anything else for you to do, is there? But I'll be cleared at the trial.'

Weather's face cracked into a grin as he said: 'You always were a fair-minded sort of chap, Brown. Even if you hadn't done it, I suppose you'd hang yourself in view of the evidence, if you were your own judge and jury.'

'I probably would,' agreed the young doctor with a smile. 'But, joking apart, this looks bad for me. I think I'd better get in touch with my lawyer, hadn't I?'

Weather said: 'No, I don't think you need do that just yet. The man who killed Natalie Dewitt made one bad slip.' The superintendent fumbled for a cigarette. 'Doctor, will you be good enough to light my cigarette for me?'

'Certainly,' nodded Brown. He took out his lighter, thumbed it open, and flicked the wheel with his right hand. Weather purposely allowed the freshly-lighted smoke to go out again and said:

'Darn it! While you have your lighter handy, give me another light, will you?' And before Brown could quite realise what was happening, Jackson had seized the Doctor's right hand and pressed his fingers on a pad.

'Fingerprints,' he said tersely.

Brown sighed. 'Better light your own cigarette, Superintendent. I seem to be pounced on at every turn.'

'No, you light it, Brown. Use your left hand. You doctors are pretty nippy with both hands, I understand. You have to be virtually ambidextrous during operations, eh?'

Brown shrugged and tried the lighter with his left hand. The lighter dropped to the floor.

Weather said: 'That's what I wanted to know. You don't use your left hand much at all, do you?'

'Not that I know of. What are you getting at, Super?'

'The inevitable slip all murderers make. The glove which the killer put in your car with the scalpel was a left-hand glove. I'm not saying you couldn't have left it there yourself to fool us — but I don't think it likely in view of the fact that one of our suspects is left-handed.'

'You mean . . . ?' gasped Brown.

'Yes, I think you know who I mean,' agreed Weather. 'Sounds surprising in the face of his foolproof alibi, but there it is. The point is that we can't disprove that alibi, just because he happens to be left-handed and because we've found a left-handed glove. The law needs more to work on than that, Doctor. That's why I'd like to enlist your help again.'

'I'll do anything I can, Super. I'll have to if I want to be cleared. What's your plan?'

'I want to reconstruct the crime with this June Merrill at the other window, just as we think she was at the time of the murder. Now, steady on, Doctor, don't raise any objections just yet. I know, she's in a nervy state, but couldn't you give her a sedative? Something to soothe her before we start, so that she won't get worked up too much?'

The young doctor looked undecided. 'She's a nice kid. I wouldn't like to have her take any chances, Super. I could give her a sedative, as you say, but . . . well, what is your exact plan?'

'I want to put her at that window, and

for each of you in turn to re-enact the murder as it probably took place, allowing her to get a clear vision of each face. That should bring back her memory, shouldn't it?'

'It may do so, but nothing's certain with these amnesia cases. She may just have a lot of needless excitement thrust on her for nothing, Super. But if you're determined, I think perhaps it's worth a try.'

'It definitely is,' agreed the superintendent. 'Unless that girl recovers her memory and we can trap this killer, you'll most likely hang, Doctor . . . Now, for the time being I want it thought that we're holding you. We will, in fact, hold you. Will you back me up to that extent?'

'It'll be rather a shock to my doting patients when they learn I'm in prison and charged with all kinds of mayhem, but I guess I'll have to cooperate, Super . . . When do you want this little party to take place?'

'I'd say as soon as it can be arranged. When will the girl be fit to undertake the job?'

Brown pursed his lips. 'Oh, if she has to do it at all, it can't harm her any more tomorrow than it would in a few weeks, when there may be less chance of her remembering. But how *about* the girl? If I'm to be held, where will she stay? I suppose Scotland Yard will want her under their protective wing.'

Weather smiled trustingly at the doctor. 'I don't think that's necessary. There's no reason why she shouldn't remain at your home, Doctor; unless, of course, you object to that arrangement.'

'Not at all. She's welcome to stay as long as she likes. I'm partial to having pleasant young girls around my home whether I'm there or not.'

Weather laughed. 'I bet you are. Perhaps, when everything is cleared up, you'd like to give her a rather different life sentence, eh?'

'Perhaps I would,' replied Brown, smiling, but behind the smile there was a hint of seriousness. 'Now, suppose you give me full instructions, Superintendent.'

★ ★ ★

'I tell you, I'll have no part of it,' raved Anthony Fulton, glaring at Jackson, who stood in the bedroom doorway. 'Having a man dragged here late at night to take part in some crazy actin', when the murderer is already arrested; it's monstrous. I'll speak to the Assistant Commissioner. He's a friend of mine; he'll make a song and dance about this.'

'I shouldn't get excited, sir,' said Jackson calmly. 'The Assistant Commissioner knows about it already. In fact, he's in the other room now with the girl who witnessed the murder. Perhaps you'd like to have a word with him.'

'But it's — it's so futile,' went on Tony Fulton. 'I mean to say, would any jury hang a man on the testimony of a woman who's hysterical and half-insane? Ridiculous! According to the newspapers, June Merrill may not have seen anything at all of the actual crime.'

Jackson shrugged.

'If you're quite innocent, Mr. Fulton, you haven't anything to worry about.'

'I'm not worrying, blast you. I'm simply saying it's shocking bad form to drag innocent people into an affair like this. It's the principle of the thing that's so foul.'

Jackson said: 'Don't you want the murderer discovered, sir?'

Fulton subsided and scowled at his toes when the chorus was taken up by Gus Barrows, who said, 'Well, I agree with Mr. Fulton. You've got the man you want. Why not let it go at that?'

Cicely Fairbarn clung on to Fulton's arm and nodded. 'It does seem so macabre — and pointless, too.'

Tom Archer, eyes gleaming, rasped: 'If there's any doubt about it, let's have the truth. Why should you all be afraid to go through with it if you're quite sure Brown did it? Apparently, the police want extra evidence before Brown is sent to trial. I'm game, Inspector.'

'Good. Then you can go first, Mr. Archer. As you can see, the scene is set as it was on the night of the murder. The young lady who takes the late Miss Dewitt's part happens to work for the police, so you needn't be afraid of scaring her. Just take the scalpel, move towards the bed, pretend to cut her throat, then stare out of the window at the flat opposite. That's all.'

Gradually the grim cameo began to take shape. Archer was the first to play the role of the murderer. He was pale, but calm. His step faltered once. Then it was soon over and he was back at the door.

Jackson said: 'All right, Mr. Fulton. We'll take you next.'

Fulton looked as if he was about to explode, but without a word he took the scalpel and moved towards the bed. His hands trembled as he made the motions of cutting the policewoman's throat, but when he returned to the others he was composed and cool again.

Gus Barrows was rather nervous over the whole thing; he took a considerable time in going through the routine. Cicely Fairbarn was even worse. She sobbed, and then dropped the scalpel from her shaking fingers. She was holding tight to the shreds of her self-control so that she would not faint.

The porter, Harry, who was also among the suspects, went through the motions mechanically, chewing vigorously at a wad of gum all the time, and even emitting a coarse whistle as he bent over the girl in the bed. Then came the turn of Suzanne, whose features clearly showed the turmoil her mind was in. Like a woman in some evil dream, she took the scalpel from Jackson, and, with faltering steps, began to cross the room.

To her, every step seemed a mile; the walls danced and swayed about her; her lips trembled, and her knees felt like jelly. She was only halfway towards the bed when her legs buckled and she thumped floorwards.

Jackson and Brown dashed to the maid's side and pulled her back, making her comfortable on the settee which stood in the other room.

'She'll be all right,' Brown said. 'It's just strain. She was fond of her mistress.'

Suzanne's eyes were already blinking open: 'I — I can't — can't — '

She broke off, seeing Jackson's staring face.

'You can't what?' said Jackson, urgently.

The maid shook her head dazedly.

'Please — don't make me do it again. I couldn't bear it. It was so — so real.'

Jackson said: 'All right, miss. But you'll have to answer a few questions. What were you trying to tell us?'

'N-nothing.'

Inspector Jackson looked heavenwards and then signalled to Brown, who took his turn quite calmly, holding the scalpel with practised ease. Barrows muttered: 'It's plain who did it. Look how he handles that damned knife. Look at the nerve he's got. Not a tremor.'

Brown, his little exhibition over, came back and sat on the edge of the settee. Jackson said: 'Now, you may as well all take it easy. The superintendent will be here shortly to tell us the worst.'

They waited in grim silence. Every face was tense and strained — all except Brown's and Jackson's. The doctor and inspector stood by the door, chatting inaudibly, as if nothing shattering was about to happen. Minutes ticked away, and Fulton rose to his feet, ready to indulge in another indignant outburst.

But at the pressure of Cicely Fairbarn's

fingers on his arm, he fought his anger and sat down again.

Steps could be heard coming up the passage. The room door opened.

Weather walked in.

He didn't speak right away, but stood glancing round at the suspects. Every face was now a frozen mask. Every eye was fixed expectantly on Weather.

Then the superintendent said tersely: 'The girl remembers nothing.'

There was a long drawn-out sigh. Weather went on: 'She doesn't even remember whether she had seen a man commit the murder. Can't even recall her own room number and the work she did for a magazine. I'm afraid you've been troubled for nothing, and I apologise. But it was well worth a trial.'

Fulton stood up and said: 'I knew quite well it was all foolery. I suppose we can go now, eh?'

'Very well. But we'll have to go on holding Brown on the murder charge. At the same time, I must ask you not to leave town until you have permission. There is a strong chance that Miss Merrill will still recover her memory.'

Brown interrupted: 'There is no necessity to move her anywhere else. She may as well remain in my home, since she won't be feeling like returning to her own flat again just yet. Mrs. Higson will look after her during the day while I'm in cussed custody.' The doctor gave a wry smile. 'Is that agreeable to you, Super?'

'Yes, I see no objections to that arrangement. I don't think Miss Merrill will, either.'

The suspects began to drift out. When all except Jackson and Weather had left, the superintendent turned to Dr. Brown with a smile. 'I think I fooled 'em, didn't I?'

'I imagine so. They couldn't have any reason to doubt your word. The only thing that worries me is June's safety. You're sure she'll be well guarded?'

'She will. There'll be four men on the job from tonight onwards.'

Dr. Brown said: 'Then she should be safe enough . . . Tell me, Super, what really happened over there?'

'Everything was grand. Her memory's

quite restored. She spotted the man as the killer the moment he came into view with that scalpel.'

'And that was — ?'

'Yes, it was the man we suspected. The left-handed merchant. Well, we've set our trap, and in a few days we'll be able to spring it. Let's hope it works.'

Brown echoed his hope fervently.

7

Girl versus Madman

'Hope you've been quite comfortable,' said Weather, his face cracking into a grin as Dr. Brown was shown into his office.

'It's been a rest cure.' The young doctor smiled. 'The boys made me quite at home, even to the extent of taking three pounds off me in a poker game. I think they cheated, Superintendent. You should pick your men with more discrimination.'

Weather grinned again and said: 'Well, you won't have to stay here much longer, Brown. I sent for you to tell you the trap's about ready to be sprung.'

It was a full week after the re-enacting of the murder scene by the suspects. Life had gone on pretty much as usual, except for Brown and June Merrill. The doctor remained on Yard premises, out of reach of nosey reporters, and to all intents and purposes in custody. June had stayed on alone at Brown's home, Weather having arranged some small details which contributed to her peace of mind.

Dr. Brown asked the superintendent: 'Has anything fresh turned up in the last week?'

'Nothing that really helps us. In fact, the only thing of any importance at all tends to confuse the issue rather than straighten it out. A constable who passed the building where Natalie Dewitt had her flat says he observed a car standing outside with engine running at ten minutes to twelve on the night of the murder. He noticed the registration number and jotted it down, meaning to report the matter and have the owner reprimanded.'

'And you traced the car?'

'Yes; according to the number the constable gave, the car must have been yours, Doctor.'

'But it couldn't — not at ten to twelve. I was driving round Westminster then. I remember looking up at Big Ben.'

Weather looked stumped. He fiddled with a paperweight and said: 'This is what

I've planned. Tomorrow, I'm arranging for the papers to print that June Merrill is slowly recovering her memory. They will make a great play of saying that this means she will be able to point out the real culprit. *Murder Secret Locked in Woman's Mind* — that sort of headline. The killer knows darned well she saw him; she told me he looked right at her, and actually came for her to finish her off.'

'Poor kid.'

'Yes, she's had a tough time of it . . . Well, as I see it, the killer will get panicky when he thinks he runs a risk of exposure. He'll lose his nerve and take steps to put her out of his way. He won't realise what we know: that, in the light of the overwhelming evidence against you, the girl's word wouldn't carry the conviction needed to sway a jury — nor would it be strong enough to crush his alibi. The only way we can do that is to trip him up: catch him out in the act of removing the solitary witness who could testify against him.'

'Can I be in at the end of the game?'

the doctor asked. 'I want to keep an eye on June Merrill.'

'That's why I've sent for you. From tomorrow night we can expect developments at any time. I've sent Jackson personally to warn the suspects to hold themselves in readiness for further questioning at any moment. That's by way of starting a doubt in the killer's mind. Tomorrow, when the papers come out, the doubt will become a fear — a fear of the gallows, and the hangman adjusting the noose, and oiling the trapdoor. I wouldn't be in that fellow's shoes for all the whisky in Scotland.'

The office door opened, and a greatly excited Jackson burst in upon them.

'Good grief, Jackson!' said Weather annoyed. 'Don't you ever knock before you enter a room?'

'But Super — '

'*Some* people have absolutely no idea of what the word privacy means,' Weather rumbled on. 'Just because you happen to be assisting me on — '

'But Super — you don't understand — she — she isn't there. The girl — the maid — Suzanne. She's vanished.'

Weather started from his chair with a startled glance at Brown. 'What happened?'

Jackson babbled on: 'I went round, warning them all there's to be further questioning shortly. The maid didn't stay at her mistress's place after the murder. She moved to a cheaper hotel in Bloomsbury. I went there looking for her. Her room was empty, but all her clothes were scattered about, and I asked the hotel manageress if she knew what time the girl would be back. She told me she didn't. It seems the maid left the place about lunchtime the day before yesterday, and hasn't been back since. That's queer, isn't it — especially as I found quite a sum of money among her belongings?'

'Aye, it is odd,' agreed Weather tiredly. 'Why in heaven's name didn't you have the sense to foresee something like this . . . ? Ah, well, I reckon it's too late now to put a man to watch the hotel. She may come back. If she does, don't let her alone for a minute until this business is cleared up. Meanwhile, circulate the usual description to all police stations, have men at all railway stations, and don't neglect airports and shipping lines. There's a slight possibility she may have left the country — if,' he added grimly, 'she's able to walk and breathe.'

But their closest enquiries failed to trace the missing maid. Brown, knowing what he knew, hadn't thought they would find her. As for Weather, he tried hard not to blame himself unnecessarily. If the girl had landed herself in any trouble — well, it was her own lookout. She had been playing with fire.

⋆ ⋆ ⋆

All newspapers the following evening carried heavy-type headlines on their front pages, relating to the murder of Natalie Dewitt. One example read starkly:

WITNESS TO MURDER
REGAINS MEMORY!

The item was read by all the suspects with mixed feelings.

Gus Barrows, still busy trying to find a dancer to replace the murdered Natalie, viewed it as a further hindrance to his efforts.

Cicely Fairbarn was chilled by the account of the disappearance of the maid rather than by the information that June was recovering.

Tom Archer read it dully, without much interest. Life had lost a great deal of its delight for him since Natalie had been killed.

Harry, the porter, said: 'Gorblimey!'

Dr. Brown smiled approval to Superintendent Weather, who said: 'Let's hope the trick'll work.'

Anthony Fulton read it with growing alarm. He sat tensely, restless fingers crumpling the edges of the newspaper. Then he rose and crossed to the telephone and dialled a number.

'Is that the residence of Dr. Brown?' Fulton asked.

'Yes,' said a girl's voice. 'Who's speaking, please?'

'It's a rather confidential matter,' said Fulton evasively. 'Who's that?'

'June Merrill.'

Fulton tensed himself. When he spoke into the mouthpiece again, his tone implied that he had never heard of the girl who had been hitting the headlines so sensationally.

'Are you the doctor's receptionist, Miss Merrill?'

'No, I don't work for the doctor. I'm a guest here.'

'I see. In that case, may I speak to someone else? His housekeeper, or one of the other servants?'

'I'm afraid not. I'm alone here at the moment. Mrs. Higson left an hour ago, and isn't due back until tomorrow morning.'

'Oh, I see. In that case, I'll ring again tomorrow. Thank you. Goodnight.'

Fulton hung up and then sat in a chair, rubbing his chin. There was no telling how soon that girl might recover. Already she seemed quite rational. He had to do something at once before it was too late.

He fortified his nerves with a long drink, then moved towards a corner bookcase. From behind the first row of novels, he extracted a narrow, waterproof case of pliant black leather. He opened it, glanced inside, then slipped it into his breast pocket.

From the same hiding place he took two strips of cloth, dyed black, except for white letters and numbers along the middle. He placed these in his coat pocket and left the house, wearing a long, dark evening coat, and a wide-brimmed hat pulled low over his eyes. Before he drove his car from the garage, he fixed the strips of numbered cloth over the front and back number plates, knowing that in the darkness they would pass for the genuine registration plates. Then he drove rapidly towards Dr. Brown's home, telling himself that if he hurried, the girl would be alone in the house.

Meanwhile, June Merrill paced restlessly up and down the library of Dr. Brown's house. That 'phone call had told her danger was on the way. She already knew who the killer was, and that it was essential to trap him the hard way.

There was bound to be a certain amount of danger: a man of Fulton's type was unpredictable . . . but every precaution had been taken, and nothing would make her back out now.

For the hundredth time she unclasped her handbag, making sure the .22 they had given her was there. She didn't know how to use it properly. Weather had instructed her, but she felt sure she'd never have nerve enough to pull the trigger. But then, perhaps the need wouldn't arise. If she did have to shoot, no doubt she could manage it in an emergency. She paced the room, wondering what Fulton would say or do. Would he be insane enough to try to do the thing right here in the flat? She shuddered.

The doorbell jarred against her thoughts. It was Fulton. She knew him in spite of the dark hat and the long, concealing coat. She stepped back, pretending surprise, and admitted him. He pushed past her, turned, and swung the door shut, saying:

'I've come here on my own initiative, Miss Merrill, because I believe you're in great danger.'

June shivered. 'We can't talk here, Mr.

Fulton. Will you come along to the library?'

He glanced about him warily, his eyes like a hunted animal. 'You're alone here?'

She nodded. 'Quite alone.'

'That's just what I was afraid of, Miss Merrill.' He followed her into the library. 'I'm afraid I've got some shocking news for you. Dr. Brown's escaped.'

'What?' The girl let her hand fly to her throat in confusion. 'When did it happen?'

'Only a few minutes ago. I chanced to be up at the Yard with Superintendent Weather when the news came in. I don't want to alarm you, but Weather is convinced Brown will make his way here to try and kill you.'

The girl looked stunned. So he was being clever. Well, it was up to her to react in the way he expected.

'Kill me? But why?'

'Because, when your memory returns, you will provide the last link in the chain of evidence which will hang him.'

'Then — then why haven't I been told of this, Mr. Fulton? Why didn't Scotland

Yard send men over to protect me?'

'Weather believes that your presence here will draw Brown, and that when he comes, they will be able to recapture him before he harms you. That is why I hurried down — to warn you myself, and to advise you not to trust too much to the superintendent and his men. They want evidence for conviction at any cost — and they're prepared to let you take the risk. You've got to get away quickly.'

June tightened her hands. She was realising, with dread, that she might have been taken in by this plausible killer if she hadn't known the truth. She forced an impression of gratitude, despite her anxiety.

'What — what can I do?'

Fulton stood up masterfully. 'I have that all solved for you, Miss Merrill. You must trust me. You see, I've arranged a hiding place for you. It's at Chippingley, about fifteen miles outside London. You're more than welcome to the use of Fulton Lodge until Dr. Brown is put behind bars again.'

She had to play for time.

'It's very kind of you, but — I really don't think — '

'Nonsense. Just slip your coat and hat on now. I can collect your other things for you later. I have my car outside, waiting.'

The girl's eyes were looking past him, through the library door into the hall, towards the dark staircase. As she gazed, a small green light winked on and off. She said immediately:

'I'll get ready at once, Mr. Fulton.'

8

His Way with Women

It was a mad drive down to Chippingley.
Fulton — having, as he thought, trapped
the girl into going with him — was now
bent on putting the rest of his plan into
effect at once. Accordingly he clamped
his foot hard on the accelerator and raced
the car at a brisk fifty miles an hour
towards Chippingley.

Twenty minutes saw them in a long,
leafy lane. The Lodge was, as Fulton had
told her, grey and gloomy, and had clearly
been unused for some time. It stood
behind high, rustic-style walls which were
trailing with ivy. A pair of wrought-iron
gates opened to the drive. Fulton climbed
from the car to open these, and after
driving in, shut them again behind him.
June welcomed these few seconds' grace,
praying that there had been no slip-up in
Weather's plan, and that she had not

merely dreamt that green signalling light in the hall at the doctor's.

Fulton parked the car in the shadow of the half-stucco, half-wood Lodge, and beckoned her out. 'You'll be quite safe here, Miss Merrill. Come along inside and I'll show you round.'

His placid charm made her feel creepy, but she pretended to be taken in by his courteous manner.

With an almost terror-stricken intensity, June hoped Weather had kept his part of the bargain. There was no way of knowing — yet. First of all, she must try and draw Fulton out: get him to admit to the murder of Natalie.

Now that June was completely in his power, Fulton's air of chivalry was fading. He took her arm and pulled her almost roughly into a chair whilst he occupied himself with lighting an oil lamp nearby.

'I haven't used the place for so long, that I didn't think it was really worthwhile to have electricity installed,' he said chattily. 'I should have done eventually, because I had intended to use this as a little love-nest for Natalie and I when we were married. A hideout where we could be away from friends — you know the sort of place.'

'Y-yes, I understand,' she gulped.

'Of course, now Natalie's dead, it doesn't matter. That's why I'm putting the hideout to another use, you see. Nobody knows I own it. It isn't large — just this one ground floor room, and two curtained bedrooms above it. Log-cabin style, and all that. Oh, yes — there's a loft over the bedrooms, which no one would ever suspect was there.' His tone became suddenly grim. 'That's where you're going, Miss Merrill!'

'I — I don't understand, Mr. Fulton,' she faltered.

'Don't you?' His eyes held a fanatical gleam. 'You soon will understand me, Miss Merrill. And you won't be lonely up there, you know. Suzanne will be in good company too. But you don't know I killed Suzanne, do you? You don't know that if your memory had returned, I am the man you would have named as the murderer of Natalie Dewitt!'

'You?' she gasped, shuddering. 'You

couldn't have done it. You must be joking.'

He chuckled shortly. 'I assure you, Miss Merrill, that I really am an exceptionally clever killer.'

'But how could it have been you? You had an — an alibi.'

'That was clever, too. I suppose I ought to tell you all about it, oughtn't I? It's traditional for murderers to tell their intended victims all about their other misdeeds, isn't it? Not that I'm traditional — but they say that most criminals are boastful and egotistical, and I suppose, for the sake of convention, I ought to run to type.

'Well, this killing business began after Suzanne told me the truth about Natalie, backed up by proof — love letters from Archer, one of Natalie's cavaliers. I had wanted to rid myself of Natalie for some time, and this gave me the chance I had waited for. I met her outside the theatre that night and told her I wanted to break off our engagement. I told her what I knew about Archer, and I demanded back some very indiscreet letters I had written her. In fact, there was quite a scene outside the stage door. It ended with Natalie swearing never to give me back my letters, and to sue me for every penny. I didn't like that. For the first time I saw right through her, and knew she'd been after my money all the time.

'Well, I'm a bit of a swine myself as you now know. I've always had a cruel streak. As a kid I was always a swine to animals, and to other boys and girls weaker — or smaller — than I was. The cruel instinct never left me, and that night it came back in full force, so that I knew I must kill her. The maid had said in her letter to me that she was betraying Natalie because she had not only detested the woman personally, but also because she had taken a great liking to me. I don't know what I'd done to deserve this; I had only spoken to her four or five times while on visits to Natalie. Anyway, she'd obviously fallen for my good looks, so I'd have been a fool not to use her, wouldn't I?

'I telephoned her that night and asked her to come round to my place. I told her I'd marry her like a shot if only I could

105

get rid of Natalie. We kissed and cuddled before I broke the news gently that Natalie must be eliminated if I wasn't going to be ruined. Suzanne was shocked at first, but after a few more cuddles, she was ready to do anything for me. Not that she had to do much — only alibi me.

'Then I left my rooms secretly, and made my way to Natalie's flat. I wanted to wait round and see how the land lay. I meant to shoot her, and so I carried a gun. When I arrived, however, I was in time to see Dr. Brown just leaving his car, and since I knew Natalie had collapsed on the stage that night, I felt sure he must be calling on her. It was then I thought of a plan to shift the guilt on to him! That was the master stroke, Miss Merrill.

'I took a note of his car number plates, and hurried back to my rooms. Then, while I fumbled through some old medical kit, Suzanne cut two strips of cloth from a pillow case. I got her to paint on them in ink, so that in a few minutes they were numbered like the plates on Brown's car. Then I took out my own car, having found just what I wanted — a case of scalpels — and tied the fake numbers over my own plates.

'When I came back, Brown had gone. I went upstairs and found Natalie in bed, reading more of those letters from the man called Archer. I demanded my own letters back. If she had only given them to me, she could have saved her life even then. But she wouldn't. So I killed her. You saw me, didn't you? Not pulling the curtains together was my one inevitable slip, which is supposed to happen in every perfect murder. Well, I panicked and tried to catch you. When my car reached the main road, I saw you lying on the ground beside Brown's car, and joining the little knot of onlookers, I learnt you'd lost your memory. That was a stroke of luck for me. After that, I carried on as I'd originally planned. I followed Brown to his home, waited until he had carried you inside, then slipped the bloodstained glove and scalpel into his car pocket, hoping it would be discovered. That completed everything. If your memory did not return, I was safe because I had timed my arrival at Natalie's to correspond with the time when Harry, the porter, would be away for his supper; and I had left again before he had come back.

'I don't mind admitting it, I had an attack of nerves when the police wanted to reconstruct the crime. But, as it turned out, all went well, and I still had my alibi in Suzanne, who was prepared to swear anything for me.'

Fulton shrugged elaborately, and went on:

'Pity about Suzanne! She should have known I hadn't meant what I'd said about marriage. I spent a few evenings with her after the murder and gave her money. But she began to object to the way I was taking too much interest in Cicely Fairbarn. Once, she even threatened to give me away to the police. That's why, just like you, I lured her down here, and, well — disposed of her. She's up in the loft with a nasty wound in her throat. Very nasty. It was inflicted with *another* of these little things!'

June was horrified as Fulton drew from his inside pocket a small leather case and tipped its contents onto the table. Three glittering scalpels lay there. He said: 'A memento of my student days, Miss Merrill, when I planned to become a surgeon. They're sharp, you know . . . Dear me, yes! *You* wouldn't guess just how sharp they are, my dear, until you've felt one, *biting into that white throat of yours . . .*'

She didn't speak, but kept staring at the scalpels in fascinated terror. They were like tiny, glittering snakes, ready to strike . . . He took one, drew it along his thumb edge, and said:

'No one knows where you've gone; no one will ever know. Don't you think I'm clever? I'm not really a professional murderer. Only an amateur. But there's a lot to be said for killing, isn't there?' His eyes were staring like a madman's. 'I find it gets a grip on you and becomes a habit. I've grown quite to like murdering people, you know. It makes you feel powerful, omnipotent. It's all so easy. When Brown hangs, there won't be a breath of suspicion against me. But come, Miss Merrill. I really have to get back to my rooms as soon as I can, in case any enquiries are made for me.'

His stiff, almost puppet-like, attitude dropped away from him. He began to advance round the table towards her. She shouted, suddenly:

'Doctor — *Superintendent!*'

'All right, Fulton,' Weather's voice cracked across the room. 'You can drop that scalpel now.'

Fulton didn't even turn. In that split-second, he realised the trap he had walked into. Since the game was up and he was to hang anyway, he threw himself, snarling, towards the girl, scalpel glittering in the lamplight, intent on making his last killing —

At the same moment, Brown appeared at the head of the wooden staircase and fired from the hip ... Fulton lurched forward with a choking cry.

⋆   ⋆   ⋆

'We had a microphone hidden in Dr. Brown's library, and two men upstairs listening in with a hastily-erected short-wave transmitter,' explained Weather to the assistant commissioner. 'As soon as Fulton told the girl where he meant to take her, they got in touch with Brown, me, and four more men who were waiting in a fast car. We got down to Chippingley well ahead of his nibs, burst in the rear door, and took up our positions, the idea being for us to get a fully detailed description of the murder before we stepped in.'

His superior smoothed his white hair.

'But how did the girl know she would be quite safe?'

'Simple. We had a small green light fixed at the top of the stairs in the Doctor's home. When that flashed, she knew we'd get details of where he was taking her, and that we were on our way.'

'Suppose that'd been a blind? If he'd taken her somewhere else — what then?'

'I'd given her a gun, and instructions on how to use it.'

After a few more remarks, Weather left the office. Outside he met Jackson.

He said: 'How's Fulton?'

'I'm pleased to say he's getting better. The shots didn't penetrate the lungs, and he'll live. So he'll know the pleasure of hanging after all.'

Weather nodded absently. 'By the way, Jackson, I've got an invitation for you to a party.'

'Party, sir?'

'Exactly. At Brown's home. An engagement party. I don't need to tell you whose, do I?'

Jackson gave him a broad wink and smiled: 'No, I don't think you do, Super! Dr. Brown and Miss Merrill will make a smashing couple.'

Message From
a Stranger

1

A Message in Lipstick

The girl at the corner table had telegraphed him a message with her eyes — some kind of an appeal. Of that, Mike Carr was positive.

She was lovely — lovely with a radiant beauty that had drawn his gaze as irresistibly as a magnet attracts steel. Try as he would, he could not help but stare.

Her hair had first attracted his attention: under the diffused glow of the ceiling lighting, it had the sheen of burnished gold. Once, when she had turned towards him, his heart had given a queer thump because he had thought he had seen recognition dawning in her eyes; for the moment, he had thought she was going to smile at him. Abruptly, she had turned back to her companion. But that one look had stamped a vision on his memory for ever — a vision of eyes so blue they seemed to probe the depths of his soul, and a mouth more lovely and inviting than anything he had ever known.

'Of course she doesn't know me,' he told himself. 'I know perfectly well I've never seen her before tonight.'

Her white gown was simplicity itself — every fold of it was moulded to her perfect figure. But such simplicity was the work of an artist, and Mike knew that even if he searched London, Paris and New York, he would not find an equal. Here, at last, was a unique woman. He forced himself to look at the girl's companion. He decided at once that he disliked him, mainly because he was far too handsome and well-dressed. Only Savile Row could have turned out such a dinner suit. But Mike had to be honest with himself: there were no signs of weakness in the other's good looks. The slightly hooked nose was predatory, and he sensed that the rather full lips could become hard and cruel.

'Women must fall for him like nine-pins,' Mike reflected. 'And, as soon as they fall, I bet he breaks their hearts.'

He turned and looked at his own rugged features in a nearby mirror. Nobody could ever accuse him of being handsome. He smiled as he reflected rather bitterly that he would stand no chance with the lovely girl at the corner table. Yet that smile did wonders to his face. Many women had declared that Mike Carr was almost handsome when he smiled. But those women did not know that Mike also smiled when he was angry, and there were those who, having seen that smile and lived, carried the memory of it with them as a constant nightmare.

Mike looked at the girl again and cursed his luck. After two years' investigating work on the Continent, he had returned to London only the day before. He had confidently expected a few months of holiday, but instead he had walked right into a new job. He would get cracking on it first thing in the morning, and goodness only knew where it would take him. If it hadn't been for this latest assignment, he would have moved heaven and earth to get to know the girl.

'Work and pleasure don't mix,' he

growled. 'What a holiday I could have had — with her!'

The girl's left hand went to her hair for a moment, and he caught the gleam of a large diamond. So, she was engaged to be married — probably to her companion. He was obviously in love with her; not for a single moment did his eyes leave her face.

A waiter approached the corner table. He evidently carried a message, for the girl's companion got to his feet, murmured an apology, and then strode quickly out of the dining-room.

Mike felt himself tempted. Should he go to her table and attempt to claim a previous acquaintanceship? The chances were he would be horribly smacked down. But it would be worth it, for at least he would hear her speak, and he badly wanted to know if her voice was in keeping with the rest of her.

His chance vanished almost as soon as it came. Two men whom he had never seen before crossed to her table. He saw her start of surprise when they sat down. One of them murmured something, and immediately the girl was as still as any frozen statue. The newcomer went on speaking, but no murmur of his voice reached Mike. After a while, the girl nodded and then reached for her lipstick. She touched up her lips, looked into a hand mirror, and then applied the lipstick again.

It was as she replaced the lipstick in her handbag that she looked directly at Mike. The glance made him start, for the vivid blue eyes were now clouded with an anxious appeal. For a moment she held his gaze — then she looked down at the table, only to turn immediately to him again.

Never had Mike been more certain. The beautiful stranger had tried to telegraph a message — a message of appeal. But surely that was absurd. This was London's most exclusive restaurant — nothing sensational could happen here.

The man who had been talking seemed to issue a command. The girl inclined her head and then rose to her feet. The second man placed his hand in his pocket for a moment and again Mike started. Had he caught a glimpse of a gun? Had a gun actually been pointed at the girl under cover of the table?

With the two men on either side of her, the girl started across the dining-room and she made no further attempt to look at Mike. For the moment he thought his imagination was playing tricks. He must have misread the look in her eyes. Yet why had she looked so pointedly at the table?

His hand moved across the tablecloth and he flicked his middle finger. His menu skidded into the air to slide underneath the newly-vacated table. Mike got to his feet and went after it. He picked up the card and then looked down at the table.

He had not been mistaken. In the interval between making up her lips, the girl had used her lipstick to write on the tablecloth. '*49b?*' queried Mike. 'What on earth does *49b* stand for?'

He went back to his table — his brow a heavy frown. *49b?* Strangely enough, it did strike some chord in his memory. He had heard the number before. But where?

Frantically, he beckoned a waiter, and pressed two pound notes into the man's surprised hand.

'I'm in a hurry,' he said. 'Keep the change.'

People turned their heads as he ran from the room. Mike thanked his stars he had used his car that night, and that he had parked it in a nearby side-street. Within a few minutes of leaving the restaurant, he was headed for Windmere Mansions.

Yes, that was it! 49b, Windmere Mansions. That was where Jennifer Weston lived. So the beautiful girl was Jennifer Weston! Despite his anxiety, Mike almost hugged himself. Jennifer Weston was very much concerned with his new job of work.

As he threaded his way through the traffic, he went over all the details of his interview with Sir Redvers Trever that morning. The Chief of the British Secret Service had been a very worried man.

'There's no holiday for you, my son,' he had said. 'You've got to find Professor

Weston, and you've get to find him at once.'

But Mike had been given very little to go on. Professor Weston was a scientist, famous in the field of atomic research. Recently he had been working on the creation of an electronic ceiling — a ceiling that would render a town or village immune from any airborne atomic bomb. It was said that the professor had succeeded in his quest — and, having succeeded, he had disappeared.

'There is no doubt he's been kidnapped,' Sir Redvers had declared. 'Unscrupulous men of any nation would commit countless murders for the chance of getting possession of such a secret. So far, we have not unearthed a single clue. But I'd like you to start fresh without any help from me. This case has got to the stage when it needs someone with an entirely unbiased mind. There are two people you must contact — Neil Rawson, the professor's chief assistant; and Jennifer Weston, his daughter. She worked as her father's secretary, and I believe she knows more about the invention than anyone else. Rawson is staying for the moment at the Garrick Hotel, and the girl is living at her flat at 49b, Windmere Mansions. After you've seen them, you can come back to me for any further information you need, but I'm hoping you'll pick up some kind of a clue for yourself.'

Life's queer, Mike thought. He had intended to have one night of liberty before tackling the case, and almost the first woman he had seen had been Jennifer Weston.

He wondered if she had recognised him. Perhaps Sir Redvers had shown her a photograph. When she had first looked towards him, he had thought he had seen recognition in her eyes. It must be so. It explained her look of appeal and the reason she had scrawled her flat number on the tablecloth.

'A young woman with brains,' decided Mike, 'and a plucky 'un as well. It took nerve to scrawl that message if they were menacing her with a gun underneath the table.'

He wondered how the girl's dinner

companion had taken her absence. The chances were that he was now running round tearing out his hair.

Before leaving Sir Redvers, Mike had asked many questions about Windmere Mansions, and had even made his chief draw a rough sketch. This was because Sir Redvers had told him a fire escape ran by the window of the girl's sitting-room.

'I like to be aware of these things,' Mike had said. 'Who knows? I may need to visit the flat when she's not at home.'

Windmere Mansions were some little way down a turning off Baker Street. Mike parked his car a street away, and then saw that a large saloon was standing directly opposite the main entrance. He wondered if Jennifer Weston had travelled in it. If so, there was no time to be lost. Turning into an alleyway, he looked up at the side wall of the block. A light was burning behind a curtained window on the second floor, and outside it he could see the skeleton outline of a fire escape. Then she had returned to the flat.

Clambering over a wall, he found himself in a narrow yard. To swing himself on to the escape was easy and he raced upwards making as little noise as possible. Reaching the platform below the window he grunted his satisfaction; the curtains were of net and the whole room was open to his gaze.

As he looked his hands clenched themselves hard.

'The swine!' he mouthed. 'They haven't wasted any time.'

The two men were in the room and one of them was twirling an automatic in his fingers. Jennifer was half-sitting, half-lying on a settee as though she had been violently thrown there. Her hair was dishevelled and an angry red mark glowed vividly on her cheek.

Mike's first impulse was to go head-first through the window. He cursed himself that for once he was not carrying a gun. But then he hadn't anticipated an adventure such as this when he started out.

Another reason held him in check. It was his task to find Professor Weston, and the finding of the professor was the most important job he had ever been given.

These men who were manhandling Jennifer were probably connected with the kidnapping. They were the first clue he had been asked to find. No matter how Jennifer had to suffer, he must hold his horses meantime.

Her voice carried to him, and he realised the window was open slightly at the top.

'You're wasting your time. No matter what you do to me, you'll never succeed in making me talk. I tell you, I know nothing of my father's code.'

Mike thrilled at the determination in her voice. She was indeed a girl in a million.

The man who had done all the talking in the restaurant took a step forward.

'There's a secret safe in this room,' he snarled. 'We know that. You'll tell me where it is, or I'll rip every hair off your head.'

He reached forward as he spoke, and it was evident he had made no idle threat. Those clutching fingers were ready to tear the sheen of lovely hair.

If those fingers had actually touched

the girl, nothing would have stopped Mike going through the window. But Jennifer spoke again, no doubt playing for time.

'The safe's behind the picture to the right of the fireplace. You turn the knob three times to the right and then twice to the left. Quite simple, you see.'

The picture was lifted down to reveal the small square of a safe door. The knob was twisted as directed, and the door swung open.

'Empty!' scoffed Jennifer. 'I hope you're satisfied.'

The man at the safe turned angrily. As he did so, Jennifer swept a cushion from the settee straight into the face of the man holding the gun. He started back, and Jennifer jumped for the door. But the other man was too quick for her. His left hand caught her, swung her round, and then his right fist smashed cruelly into her face. She went down without a sound and lay in a pitiful heap on the carpet.

Mike, blind to all reason, tore his fingernails as he struggled to fling up the window. He would get into the room, and he would deal with the swine who had struck Jennifer.

A harsh-sounding voice from inside the room jerked him back to sanity.

'Give me a hand with her,' it rapped. 'There's nothing for it now but to get her to Greytowers.'

2

The Girl's Story

Grimly Mike stifled his anger. As far as he was concerned, the case was breaking wide open: everything was falling into his lap. The two crooks were taking Jennifer to a place called 'Greytowers'. He'd bet that that was the name of the house where Professor Weston was being held prisoner. If he was careful, now he would be able to follow them. Once the house was located, the rescue of the professor should be easy.

Mike swore that nobody was going to rescue Jennifer except himself. When he succeeded, she would be grateful. And, being grateful, she might yield to him.

He caught his breath. Already he had visualised Jennifer in his arms — had sensed the clinging softness of her body. His thoughts became fanciful. When he found the professor, he would be able to take his holiday; and Jennifer, being grateful to him, might be tender to him . . .

'I'm just a dumb clod!' he told himself. 'I haven't even spoken to her yet. And isn't she engaged to someone else? Act your age, Mike.'

The two crooks had wasted no time. Between them, they picked up the girl, and the man who had struck her down slapped her face in order to bring her round. Mike memorised his every feature. Soon — very soon — he was going to beat that hated face to a pulp. When he was through with him, there would be one creep in the world who would never again lift his hand to a woman.

Mike waited to see no more. Instead, he turned and darted down the fire escape. He must be right on hand when the three left the building.

Down in the yard his luck petered out. Swinging himself onto the top of the wall, he suddenly froze. A policeman was walking down the alleyway. Mike lay flat and held his breath. He thought he had been seen, because the policeman stopped directly beneath him. Instead of issuing a challenge, however, he switched on his torch and then proceeded to study his notebook by its light. Mike called him every name he could lay tongue to. He dared not declare himself. Explanations would take far too long.

It could only have been a matter of minutes, but to Mike it seemed like hours. Finally the policeman grunted, switched off his torch, and went on his way.

Mike raced out of the alleyway just in time to see a dark figure climbing into the driving seat of the big saloon. So Jennifer was already inside. And he — he was going to miss his chance — for, by the time he reached his own car, the saloon would be out of sight.

The engine revved into life and the car started to move. Mike saw something that sent him forward at speed. The saloon was fitted with an old-fashioned luggage grid. As it started to gather speed, Mike grabbed the handle of the luggage boot and swung himself onto the grid. He was scared then that the clatter of his arrival had been heard by the men inside the car.

Even now, he wasn't too happy. As the vehicle drove through the lighted streets, he was bound to be seen. There would be danger for him at every traffic block — some officious busybody was sure to inform the occupants of his presence.

Soon, however, he was congratulating himself. The car was headed north and the driver was keeping to the side streets. Mike realised the driver must be as scared of traffic blocks as he was himself. When the car turned into a wide arterial road, Mike breathed his final relief. All being well he would still be on the grid when the car reached its destination.

One thing Mike omitted to take into consideration — the need for petrol. Without any warning, there was a sudden squealing of brakes and the car turned into the lighted front of a petrol station. Even before it stopped, an attendant was striding forward.

Mike cursed his luck. There was far too much light about. If he dropped off and took to his heels, he was bound to be seen. The gang would then see to it that he never had another chance to ride on the grid. Accordingly, he did the only thing he could. Slipping off his perch, he darted to the far side of the car, and here he crouched down.

The driver climbed out and approached the attendant. He was obviously making sure the man had no chance to see inside the car.

'Give me six!' he rapped. 'Make it snappy.'

Petrol gurgled into the tank and Mike squeezed himself against the side of the car. At any moment the attendant might look round and see him. But the petrol cap was screwed on, and then he heard the attendant's voice.

'I won't be a moment getting the change,' he said.

Mike breathed again. It was going to be all right after all. The attendant might see him when he swung back onto the grid, but chances were the engine would drown any alarm that he raised.

A dark figure stepped from behind the car — the figure of the driver.

'Why, Jim,' he said, 'I didn't think — '

It was all part of the same movement. Mike catapulted upright, his right fist moving from the moment he started. It crashed full into the other's chin, and Mike's every nerve tingled with satisfaction.

The crook who had struck Jennifer had received the first instalment of what was coming to him. He sagged at the knees and then slowly crumpled up. No sound of any sort escaped him. Mike's fist had knocked him cold.

All Mike's plans had gone haywire now. He could only hope to make sure of Jennifer's safety. Speed was vital. Within a few seconds the attendant would be returning.

He moved to the side of the car and yanked open one of the doors.

'Jim!' he breathed huskily into the interior. 'Quickly!'

There was a gasp and then the accomplice came tumbling out.

'What's wrong?' he demanded. 'What — *ah!*'

He was in the act of straightening himself as Mike's fist made contact. As he slid down the side of the car, Mike clawed his way into the driving seat.

'You're in good hands, Jennifer,' he said. 'I'm taking charge.'

The engine roared into life. Then the echo of a shout reached him as he turned into the roadway.

'You've had it, brother,' he called. 'Nothing stops me now.'

He realised then that there had been no sound from the girl. Surely she was still inside the car? He turned his head and saw her lying back in the far corner.

'Jennifer,' he began. 'Er — Miss Weston — '

A faint, sickly odour assailed his nostrils. No wonder she had not spoken. Those swine had drugged her.

'Poor kid!' he murmured. 'You're certainly having a rough passage tonight. But I reckon they had to drug you — it was the only way they could be sure of keeping you quiet. I'm raising my hat to you, Jennifer.'

He turned down a side road. The chances were the two crooks would steer clear of the police — they'd be too scared to give information about the stolen car. But he wasn't taking any chances. He was going to get Jennifer to a safe place and then he was going to have a long talk with her — a very long talk.

He'd take her to the cottage. That was it. The place was a bit musty — it had stood empty so long. And he had given his man the night off, too. Still — she would be safe at the cottage.

He swung the car Londonwards, for his cottage was on the river near Kingston.

Jennifer was still unconscious when the car glided to a stop. Darting to the front door of the cottage, he unlocked it and then rushed back.

'I'm scared to leave you alone for even a moment,' he said.

Reaching inside, he gathered her limp body into his arms. There was no imagination about this — this was the real thing. Mike decided he hadn't been around when imaginations were handed out. His every nerve tingled as his arms held her close.

He carried her over the threshold — looked down at her and smiled.

'Perhaps — one day — I'll be carrying you over this threshold again,' he murmured. 'Your arms will be around my neck, your eyes will be open, and they'll be looking at me. And they — '

He shook his head impatiently at his fantasizing.

He knocked down the electric light switch with his elbow, and then tenderly placed her on the settee in the tiny sitting-room. Looking down at her, he saw she was even more beautiful than he had imagined. Her lovely mouth was slightly parted — impulsively, he bent down and pressed his lips against it.

Jennifer sighed and her eyes fluttered open. Stark horror filled them. She stared at Mike as though he was the lowest reptile that ever crawled on the earth's surface.

'*Ugh!*' She shuddered. 'I could kill you for that — !'

Suddenly her vivid blue eyes were full of relief.

'So *you're* Mike Carr,' she whispered. 'I — I thought that one of *those* — those horrible *brutes* had — had kissed me. I must have been having a nightmare.'

Mike felt hot around the collar.

'Yes, I'm Mike Carr,' he said quickly. 'I figured you recognised me in the restaurant.'

She nodded. 'Sir Redvers told me you were going to look for Father,' she told him. 'He showed me several photographs of you so that I'd be sure of you when we met. That — that's why I scrawled the number of my flat on the tablecloth when — when those horrible men were menacing me. I — I only had time to scrawl the number, but I hoped you'd — '

'Yes, I tumbled to it,' he said. 'But what actually happened?'

'Neil — he's my fiancé — was called away to the telephone. They came over and one of them pointed a gun at me under the table. They told me that if I wanted to save Dad's life, I'd have to take them to my flat.'

Mike went taut. So she was engaged to Neil Rawson — Professor Weston's chief assistant. Jennifer had probably known him for years. So he, Mike, didn't stand a celluloid cat's chance in Hades as far as she was concerned. And only a few moments ago he had been thinking, imagining how he would like to own this desirable creature.

'All Dad's notes are written in code,' she was saying. 'I'm the only other person who understands it. Well, it was the secret of the code they were trying to force out of me. Oh, they were horrible — beastly — '

'They're going to pay for it,' he assured her. 'Right up to the hilt, and then some. But if you're the only other person who knows the code, then you've got to be hidden in a place where they'll never find you. Don't worry — it won't be for long. I've a clue to your father's whereabouts, and — '

Her head went back against the cushion.

'I'm — I'm feeling faint,' she whispered. 'That — that horrible cloth they pressed over my face. If you — if you could get me a cup of tea — '

'Of course,' he said.

Suddenly there was a faint smile in her eyes.

'Mike,' she murmured, 'I'm glad it was you who kissed me!'

Mike went into the kitchen and he was treading on air. So she was glad he had kissed her! Perhaps he wasn't such a clod after all. Perhaps this was still going to be the finest holiday of his life. Maybe Neil Rawson wasn't so very important. Then he frowned: the girl had only been relieved because it might have been one of those crooks who was kissing her . . .

He filled the kettle and placed it on the stove. Taking out cups and saucers, he saw they were thick with dust. What an idiot he had been to give his man, Slug Emery, the night off. He should have made him clean up everything first of all. Still, it was lucky they had laid in a stock of provisions.

He made the tea and then stood the pot on the stove to brew. She would need it strong, so he would give it a good few minutes.

He poured the tea at last, and wondered if she would like sugar. In the act of setting the cup down again, he started — and the cup fell to the floor, its contents scalding his legs. He never even noticed the pain.

At that moment a car had suddenly started up outside the cottage.

'What on earth!'

Mike darted into the sitting room and pulled up as though he had met an invisible barrier. The settee was empty.

Jennifer had gone!

Lying on the settee was a crumpled sheet of paper. He read the message:

'Thanks for your help. I can manage by myself now.'

Still not believing it, he pulled the window curtains aside to see the rear lights of a car disappearing down the road.

'But it doesn't make sense!' he exploded. 'There was no need for her to flee. She knew she was quite safe with me, and — '

Turning from the window, his gaze suddenly focused on the carpet underneath the settee.

'I — I knew it!' he growled huskily in his throat.

Jumping to the settee, he picked up the

crumpled paper and studied the message. All the letters sloped backwards.

'Jennifer wouldn't write a hand like this,' he declared. 'It isn't a woman's writing at all — it's a man's. He's sloped the letters backwards in order to make it look like a woman's handwriting.'

He stooped then, and picked up from under the settee the thing that had held his attention. It was one of Jennifer's shoes.

She would never have fled the cottage leaving one of her shoes behind. Its presence meant that someone had carried her out of the room.

In other words, Jennifer had been kidnapped again — kidnapped from right under his nose.

3

Why Women Scream

Jennifer smiled in her sleep. She was dreaming she was back in the restaurant and Mike Carr was staring at her. She had recognised him the moment he had sat down. She had thought him unattractive from his photographs — but photographs could be dreadfully deceptive. There was something strangely appealing about his rugged features; she liked his level gaze, and she admired the strength of his chin. All in a flash, she was happier than she had been for weeks. Now that a man like Mike Carr was about to investigate her father's disappearance, the chances that the mystery would be solved had increased a thousandfold.

She had imagined the feel of his strong arms around her — had pictured the comfort and protection that such strength would give. But it was disloyal to surrender to such thoughts, for soon — very soon — she would be married to Neil.

She smiled again. She was lying on a settee and someone had kissed her. She had been both thrilled and horrified. She had thought it was the brute who had struck her. Then she had opened her eyes to see Mike. The relief had thrilled her.

Then she saw that horrible, masked face bending over her, and again an evil-smelling pad was pressed over her face.

She stirred and realised she was now lying in a car. But, try as she would, she could not open her eyes. She was still too much under the influence of the drug. She knew then that the car had stopped, but her limbs still refused to obey the dictates of her mind.

When at last she did open her eyes, she was lying on a couch in a barely-furnished room. There was a table and a chair and nothing else. The room was gloomy; turning her head, she saw that the only window was boarded up.

Desperately, she fought down panic. No matter what happened, she must keep her sanity. The men who had kidnapped her were the men who had kidnapped her father. There was nothing they would not do to obtain what they wanted. She must be brave — brave as her father had been. Although he had been their prisoner for weeks, he had refused to disclose the secret of the code. If he had done so, they would not have been interested in her. She must keep the secret just as her father had kept it. The lives of millions depended upon her. No matter what happened to her, she knew her father would still want her to keep the secret.

She was waiting for the strength to return to her limbs when she heard the sound of a heavy bolt being drawn. The door opened and her hand flew to her mouth as she fought to stifle a scream. A figure wearing a long gown entered, his face hidden behind a grotesque, square-cut mask. It was the same horrible masked figure which she had seen bending over her when she had been lying on Mike's settee.

The unknown man walked towards her with the silent grace of a tiger.

'I'm glad to see you're in a fit state to talk,' he said meaningfully. Defiantly, she stared back at him. It was impossible to see even his eyes, for the slits in the mask were too narrow.

'I don't need to tell you why you have been brought here,' the harsh voice went on. 'Your father's been my prisoner for a long time. As you know, I've got all his papers, but it so happens that they are written in code. That code has defied some of the most famous experts in the world. Despite — er — *persuasion*, your father has refused to enlighten me. I regret to inform you that he is now in a very weak state. Only you can save him from death, and you can do that by telling me the secret of the code. Accede to my request, and not only will you be given your freedom, but your father will be returned to you before the day is out.'

'You got nothing from my father,' she said softly. 'And you won't make me talk either.'

Somehow she sensed that he was

smiling behind the mask.

'You are a woman, and a woman regards many things as important. Much more so than a man. It does not matter that I have failed with your father, because I shall succeed with you.'

Cold horror crept into her veins.

'If necessary, I shall stretch those lovely limbs upon a rack,' the unemotional voice continued. 'Moreover, I can so mark that lovely face that men will shudder to look upon you. But with you, knowing that obstinacy is bred in you, the worst shall come first.'

He came a step nearer — the hideous visage bent close towards her. She knew that her face was as white as a death mask, and that her eyes were wide pools of horror.

'If — if my answer is still the same?' The question was forced from her.

He made a gesture of finality.

'You will be taken down to the men who will be waiting to torture you,' he said. 'That will be tomorrow. Tonight I'm giving you the chance to come to your senses.'

As the door closed behind him Jennifer knew that madness was close at hand. She had imagined torture — she had imagined herself defying the worst. But could she? Could she possibly live through the coming day and still keep the secret of the code? There was nothing she could do to help herself. When she tried to leave the couch, her legs gave way under her; she was still weak from the effects of the drug.

It seemed hours before she was able to drag herself round the room. She tried the door, but it was held so firmly by heavy bolts that she could not even shake it. In her panic she crossed to the fireplace and peered up the chimney, hoping against hope that she might be able to claw her way through it. But there was no hope of escape by that way.

Then she crossed to the shuttered window. It was small and square, but it would be big enough for her to squeeze through. Even if she succeeded only in forcing the shutters, she might be able to attract attention. She tried to wrench up the lower half of the window, but it was held securely by screws. In order to reach the shutters, she would have to smash the glass.

Jennifer forced herself to be cool. There was probably a guard outside the door, and he would come running at the sound of breaking glass. But somehow she had to get at the shutters. She remembered her small vanity bag. She still had it because it was attached to her wrist by a ribbon. Opening it, she took out her nail file. It was a poor weapon, but better than nothing. If she worked the end of it between the wood and the glass, she might be able to lever the whole pane away. Once that was done, she would find a means of dealing with the shutters.

Feverishly, she went to work, and her heart pounded when she realised the woodwork was rotten with age. It gave easily under pressure of the nail file.

As she worked, some sixth sense hammered in her brain. It warned her that her every action was being watched. She looked at the door, but there was no opening there, and she was out of the line of the keyhole. She told herself it was only because of her terror that she felt herself being watched.

Suddenly she was conscious of the picture behind her. It was a nondescript oil painting of the head and shoulders of a man. Looking at it closely, she suddenly saw the eyes move.

With fresh terror gripping her heart, she crossed to the picture. She must have been mistaken. She — she *had* to be mistaken; because, if those eyes had moved, then she had no possible hope of escape . . .

Gripping the picture frame, she tried to tear it from the wall. It held fast. She continued to pull — she had to make sure. Then something splashed onto her face, and she became conscious of that sickly odour she had grown to loathe.

She faltered away from the wall and reached, in groping fashion, for the couch. She — she must not let herself be drugged again. She — she had to make sure of escape. The night was coming — and — and soon it would be tomorrow . . .

She was still lying on the couch when

she opened her eyes. The room had grown much darker. Was it night already?

Jennifer lifted her head and immediately the full horror of her position burst upon her. Some of her clothes had been taken away, and she was lying on the couch with an old blanket thrown carelessly over her.

The door opened and she clutched the blanket around her. But it was a woman who entered — a hard-featured woman of uncertain age who carried a steaming cup in one hand and a rubber truncheon in the other.

Jennifer forced herself to speak.

'So you took my clothes!'

There was no expression in the woman's face.

'Yes, so you wouldn't be able to escape,' she answered. 'Here — drink this. It will clear your head and you will become strong again.'

Jennifer would have refused, but her strength was not equal to the task. She was forced to submit while the other held the cup to her lips. Only then did Jennifer realise how great was her thirst.

Her brain began to clear and she felt new strength flow into her limbs. She would have caught the other's arm, but the woman withdrew sharply.

'You — you are a woman,' Jennifer said. 'You know how they intend to torture me. You'll help me — you must help me!'

The other's face remained expressionless.

'It is because I am a woman that I have come to you,' she answered. 'No harm will befall you if you will only be sensible. Tell them what they want to know. If you refuse, then I would not be you for anything in the whole of this world.'

The temptation was terrible.

'No!' Jennifer said. 'I can't tell anything. I mustn't!'

The woman shrugged her shoulders, and then rapped on the table with her truncheon. Two masked figures entered the room.

'Take her!' said the woman.

Jennifer was still too weak to resist.

They carried her down into the cellars

and into a box-like stone chamber where they flung her callously upon a heap of rags. When they had left her, she saw no sign of any door.

Her mind was clear now, and her strength almost returned. Sharply, she realised that her greatest fight must be against insanity.

They did not keep her waiting very long. A section of the wall facing her slid back and three gowned figures entered. The centre one was the man in the grotesque mask.

Noiselessly, he glided forward, until he was bending over her as she crouched against the rags.

'The time of waiting is over,' he said. 'You have been given the respite I promised you. For the last time, I ask you to remember all that I told you this morning. If you are foolish, there is no power on earth that can save you. Remember also that your father's life is in your keeping. Are you ready to give me the secret of the code? Answer — yes or no!'

Her eyes stared back at him. This —

this was the beginning of her time of terror.

'The answer is — no!' she said, and marvelled at the firmness of her voice.

His hands reached towards her.

'Then it is *I* who will teach you your first lesson,' he said softly.

It was then that Jennifer screamed.

4

A Kiss Before Dying

Mike Carr entered the office of Sir Redvers Trevor and started at the sight of his chief's visitor. It was Jennifer Weston's too-handsome fiancé — Neil Rawson.

Sir Redvers indicated a chair.

'I'm glad to see you, Mike,' he said. 'This is Neil Rawson — Professor Weston's chief assistant. He brings me very alarming news. Oh, this is Michael Carr — the young man I've been telling you about, Rawson.'

The other ignored the introduction.

'I'm worried out of my life,' Rawson snapped. 'It's my fiancée — Miss Weston. We dined together last night, and, at the end of the meal I was called to the telephone. I understood my caller was Sir Redvers, and it was some considerable time before I found I was being deceived. On realising that fact, I returned post-haste to my table to discover that Jennifer — Miss Weston — was missing. On making enquiries, I learned she had left in the company of two strangers. Since then, there has been no news at all of her, and I — I fear the worst.'

'I know,' said Mike. 'I dined at a nearby table last night.'

Neil Rawson stared at him.

'I don't remember you.'

'I saw Miss Weston leave and I followed her,' Mike said. 'I even rescued her. But you'd better hear the whole story.'

He explained all that had happened with one single omission: he made no mention of Greytowers. At the end of it Rawson was livid.

'You — *you saved her*,' he said furiously, 'and then — then you let them take her again? I — I shall never see her again now. Why, in heaven's name, didn't you take her to the police? They would have looked after her; there would have been no second kidnapping. And — and if you're the *bungler* who's going to handle *our* case — '

'That will be *quite enough*, Rawson!' The chief's voice cut like a whip. 'Mike acted just as I would have had him act.'

He went over the points of Mike's story one by one.

'But what are we going to do?' demanded Rawson. 'We — we just can't sit here. These fiends will murder Jennifer, or worse — '

He made a frantic gesture.

'Everything that we can do, we will do,' Sir Redvers assured him. 'If you will only leave the case in our hands — '

Rawson's chair scraped back as he came to his feet.

'First Professor Weston and now Jennifer!' he said bitterly. 'I'm beginning to lose faith in police methods. But I can promise you I have no intention of sitting still. I feared something like this would happen, so I engaged a private detective to keep Jennifer under observation. He is missing this morning, so it may be he has news for me. If so, I will get in further touch with you. Good day.'

He stalked out of the room.

'That's somebody I don't like,' said Mike positively.

Sir Redvers smiled.

'We must make allowances,' he said. 'Don't forget, he's in love with Miss Weston and they're engaged to be married.'

'Yes,' gulped Mike. 'I'm not likely to forget that.'

His dream of conquest was over. The chances were that Jennifer would never look at him again. She would blame him for the second kidnapping. That was — if nothing happened to her!

'Rawson's private detective,' he pondered. 'D'you think he might have followed me — that it was he who took Jennifer from the cottage?'

'I shouldn't think so,' was the reply. 'Had he done so, he would have taken her straight to Rawson. But you have been keeping something back. I could see your anxiety to get rid of Rawson. What is it?'

Mike told him about Greytowers. The news excited Sir Redvers.

'The first clue yet,' he said. 'Your luck is something to marvel at, Mike.'

'It's not!' said Mike flatly. 'Didn't I lose Jennifer?'

Sir Redvers didn't answer. He was using his private line to Scotland Yard.

There was a long, weary wait. It was late afternoon before Sir Redvers had any real news.

'There seems to be a Greytowers in every county,' he explained, 'and we've had to check up on every one of them. Each one seems to be occupied by a family which is above suspicion. But news of a likely one has just come through.'

He looked at some notes on his writing pad.

'It's an old house near Lengley village,' he said. 'After standing empty for years, it was taken over by new tenants some few months ago. Ever since, the village has been agog with curiosity concerning the new tenants. They are never seen, and nobody is allowed inside the grounds.'

'It fits the bill,' declared Mike. 'Anyway, I'm going to make sure, and I'm wasting no time. Now, Chief, I want you to let me play a lone hand until I'm absolutely sure. I don't want to run any risks. These men are desperate, and if the police move too quickly there's no telling what they may do.'

'It's your case. This particular Grey-towers must be investigated before we turn the police on to it. I wish you luck.'

When Mike had gone, Sir Redvers shook his head sympathetically.

'A great pity the young 'un has fallen for Jennifer Weston,' he murmured. 'I didn't drag him into this case so that he could break his heart over it.'

Mike's first job was to locate his car. This was easy: he found it in safe custody at the police station round the back of Windmere Mansions. As he drove north, he knew only one regret. He would have liked to have had his man, Slug Emery, with him. Slug was a very good man to have at one's elbow when there was danger about. He prayed, too, that he was headed for the *right* Greytowers. If so, then he was headed for Jennifer.

It was dark when he reached Lengley village — darker still as he climbed a high boundary wall. He strained his eyes as he peered into the darkness. The house was somewhere ahead of him, but there were no lights to betray its presence.

His progress was painfully slow. He didn't move a yard without testing the ground before him. Whatever happened, he must beware of tripwires or anything else that had been set to give an alarm.

He came to the house at last — a gaunt pile against the darkness. Still there was no light to be seen, and his heart sank as the thought struck him that he might be on the wrong track. But, having come so far, he intended to make sure. He could only do that by forcing an entry.

All the windows on the ground floor were heavily shuttered. But, working his way round to the back, he found a small scullery window. It wasn't particularly wide, but he reckoned he would be able to wriggle through.

This wasn't the first house he had burgled, and he had no difficulty in forcing the window. It was even more of a squeeze than he had thought, but he managed to get through. As he had expected, he found himself in a scullery. The light of his torch showed him plates in a rack, and he saw that the draining-board was still damp. Someone had been in this room very recently.

Shifting the torch to his left hand, he drew out his automatic. If Jennifer was indeed inside this house, then he might have urgent need of a gun — and he would have no compunction about using it if necessary.

Mike found his way into a wide hall. No line of light showed under any of the doors, and the upstairs was shrouded in darkness. He stood motionless and strained every faculty as he listened. No sound came to him. Except for the damp draining-board, he would have sworn that the house was empty.

There was nobody on the ground floor. Of that, he was positive. Now he must search upstairs. On tiptoe he moved to the staircase. He placed one foot on the first step, and then the hair suddenly bristled on the back of his neck.

From somewhere below, a woman had screamed — and he knew it was Jennifer!

The light of his torch flashed along the side of the staircase. He saw it then — a concealed door. He pressed against it, thinking he would have to break it down, but it opened at his touch. Before him was a flight of steps leading into darkness.

Careless of the danger, he went down the stairs three at a time. The light of the torch stabbed the length of a long cellar, but he saw nobody there. Yet the faint whimper of a voice came to him, and it sounded from beyond the further wall. Here there was no sign of a door, but set in the wall was a short lever. Mike pulled on it.

Without any sound, a section of the wall slid open, revealing a hidden door, and he stood blinking in the light from a small box-like chamber. He saw three gowned figures — and then he saw Jennifer.

Her hair was dishevelled about her face, and her eyes wild with a terror that turned his blood to ice. He saw the white alabaster of her shoulders — saw that her only garment was a blanket. One of the men was brandishing a whip at her as she crouched on a bed. He went berserk then.

'I'll kill the lot of you,' he yelled frenziedly.

His finger was white on the trigger as he heard the sound behind him. He fired as he turned — caught a glimpse of the woman behind him and the uplifted truncheon. He tried to fling up an arm, but the descending weapon took him on the temple. He staggered forward into the chamber; the gun fell from his grasp, and then he pitched onto his face.

As he fell, he knew a great contempt for himself. He had failed Jennifer in her hour of greatest need.

There was a babble of voices.

A woman's voice: 'I saw him as he raced into the cellar. I hit him as soon as I could.'

The harsh voice of a man: 'Leave him! There are probably others with him. We must get back to the house. It's our only chance. Hurry!'

Mike fought unconsciousness and won. Staggering to his feet, he saw that the gowned figures and the woman had gone. There was no sign of any door — there was nothing to mark it inside the chamber.

And his gun was missing, too — they had evidently taken it from him.

He turned to Jennifer; and then, for Mike, a miracle was born. He saw the glory in her face and he saw her arms outstretched to him.

He stumbled towards her and went down on his knees.

'Jennifer! Are you all right?'

Her head cushioned against his shoulder and his arms went round her.

'I am now. But I was badly scared. It was too horrible. Then, when I'd lost hope, I saw you. Oh, Mike, you were the answer to my prayers.'

'I'm not much of an answer,' he murmured bitterly. 'I came here to rescue you. For all the good I've done, I might just have stayed away. They'll come back, and — '

She smiled up at him then — a smile completely trusting. 'They won't harm me now,' she said. 'Not now that you are here. I know that, Mike.'

Her arms gripped him tightly.

'No, they won't harm you,' he vowed. 'No matter how many of them there may be, I'm going to get you out of this. I swear it, Jennifer.' He tilted her chin. 'When you walked into that restaurant, Jennifer,' he murmured, 'I fell like a shooting star.'

'It happened to me, too, Mike,' she said softly. 'You looked so tough and dependable. When I scrawled my flat-number on the tablecloth, I knew you would understand that I needed you. You see, Mike, you're everything that I've wanted in life. Oh, darling, we have so much to give one another. But they will come back, and if — if we have to die — '

He drew her to him and he knew the sweet surrender of those lovely lips.

5

The Girl in Red

Time stood still as far as Mike was concerned. Afterwards, he never knew exactly how long Jennifer and he were left alone, kissing each other with delirious ecstasy.

But there came a moment when he thrust her behind him — when he crouched ready to spring. His lips twisted into that terrible, grim smile — more terrible than it had ever been before. The secret door had started to open. Another moment, and he would be fighting for Jennifer's life.

His forward surge stopped.

No masked figures appeared in the open doorway. Instead, he saw Neil Rawson! Behind Rawson were police helmets.

Rawson stared at him in blank surprise. 'You, Carr!' he said, and his voice was biting in its contempt. 'You're the *last person* I expected to find *here*.' He pushed Mike aside as he went down on his knees before his fiancée. 'Thank goodness I've found you, Jennifer,' he said. 'I've been terrified for your safety. I've moved heaven and earth to find you. And — and why are you in this state? What terrible things have they done to you?'

Jennifer was weeping. Deliverance had come out of the blue and now the reaction had set in.

'They've done nothing to me,' she said. 'It was Mike who stopped them.'

'And your father?' he demanded. 'Have you seen him? Where is he?'

'I know nothing of Daddy,' she said. 'I only know they've been torturing him.'

'But how did you find us?' demanded Mike.

Rawson stared at him coldly.

'I told you I'd engaged a private detective to act as Miss Weston's body-guard,' he said icily. 'Last night, he discovered that someone else was shad-owing her. So, knowing she was safe with me, he concentrated on this other shadower. And, this morning, he was led to this house. He got in touch with me, and I lost no time in coming here to see the place for myself. As soon as I'd heard some of the village gossip, I knew this was the place we were looking for. I reported at once to the local police and we've just raided the house. We found it empty. In fact I thought I'd brought the police on a fool's errand until I noticed the lever outside. I pulled it down, and, well — I found Jennifer. But tell me — were you kidnapped too?'

Mike told as much of his story as he considered necessary.

'You always did take too much on yourself,' Neil Rawson flashed at him. 'You should have gone to the police at once. Thank goodness *I* had the sense to do so.'

He turned to Jennifer.

'Your other clothes are in one of the upstairs rooms,' he said. 'As soon as you're dressed I'll take you home. Come on, dear.'

She looked at Mike.

'The sooner you're home, the better,' Mike said. 'I can't leave just yet — I'm going to explore every nook and cranny of this house before I go. There may be other torture rooms like this.'

Jennifer, the blanket wrapped tightly around her, left on Rawson's arm.

Aided by the police, Mike searched the house from roof to cellar. It was a waste of time. There was no sign of any other secret room and the masked crooks had not left a single clue behind them.

'They didn't leave much to chance,' reflected Mike. 'They must have fled the house the moment they locked me in the cellar.'

He drove back to his cottage. Slug Emery, his batman, opened the door to him.

'I'd given you up, guv,' he said. 'I was just going to bed.'

'Things have been happening,' said Mike. 'But I'm not talking about them now. I'm in need of sleep. Wake me at the usual time with an extra-large breakfast.'

He told Slug some of his adventures next morning.

'You shouldn't have left me out of it, guv,' Slug said. 'If there's any more trouble ahead I want to be in on it.'

'There's likely to be plenty,' said Mike. 'You'll get your wish.'

Slug, a first-class handyman, had reconnected the telephone. At mid-morning Mike rang Jennifer's flat.

'Can I speak to Miss Weston, please?' he said.

'This is Miss Weston's maid,' was the reply. 'She's still asleep and I don't like to disturb her.'

'Well, the longer she sleeps the better,' said Mike. 'Tell her Mr. Carr rang up and that I'll ring again this afternoon.'

The same voice answered his afternoon call.

'Miss Weston is out,' he was told. 'Mr. Rawson called for her.'

'Oh!' said Mike, and replaced the receiver.

He felt sorry for Neil Rawson then. If Jennifer had gone out with him, it could only be for one purpose. That would be to tell him that the engagement was off — that she was in love with Mike.

'He hates me already,' Mike thought. 'How he'll hate me now! I think I'll have to make lots of allowances for him in the future. Poor blighter!'

But he wished he could have caught Jennifer before she had left. He had wanted to know how, and when, she was going to tell Rawson. Actually, he had been trying to keep Jennifer out of his mind all day. If he had taken the easy way, his whole mind would have been filled with thoughts of her. But it was his job to find her father, and now he was back where he had started — with not a single clue that he could follow up.

He was racking his brains to discover a line of action when his telephone shrilled. He jumped to the receiver, thinking it would be Jennifer at the other end.

Instead, he heard the clear incisive voice of Sir Redvers Trevor.

'That you, Mike? Thank goodness you're at the cottage. Can you come into town almost at once?'

'I can,' answered Mike. 'Is there a new lead?'

'I think so,' was the reply, 'but it isn't

wise to give you any real information over the 'phone. However, this is what I want you to do. At eight o'clock tonight you must be walking down Farr Street. Approach it from the direction of the West End and keep to the right-hand pavement. A girl dressed all in red will be walking towards you. She's your contact. Give her your name, and then she will let you have some very surprising information. As usual, it's up to you to work out your own line of action after you've heard her news.'

'O.K.,' said Mike. 'I'll try not to fall down on the job this time.'

Before leaving, he rang Jennifer's flat again, only to learn that she had not returned. He hoped that she wasn't finding Neil Rawson too difficult. After that, he gave Slug his instructions for the night.

Mike went to town by train.

Farr Street, he knew, was a narrow thoroughfare off Soho — a thoroughfare that respectable people avoided after dark. A nearby clock was striking the hour as he turned into the street and started to walk along the right-hand pavement. It was a poorly-lit street, and between the lights there were wide blocks of black shadow. It was from one of these blocks that a cry suddenly came.

'Help! Oh, help!'

Mike started to run.

'Hold on!' he shouted. 'I'm coming.'

He raced into the shadow. Vaguely, he glimpsed two figures vanishing into the gloom. Then he nearly fell over a figure on the pavement.

It was that of a girl dressed all in red. As he jerked to a stop, she started to rise to her feet. 'Oh! My head!' she moaned.

He bent to give her a hand, and saw the trickle of blood on her face.

'I'm Mike Carr,' he said. 'I came here to meet you. What happened?'

She looked at him dazedly.

'I — I was walking to meet you,' she said shakily. 'They — they were waiting for me in a doorway. One of them jostled me and then the other struck me down. Oh!'

She placed a hand to her head and then

shuddered when she saw the blood on her fingers.

'Come under the light,' Mike said. 'You may be badly hurt.'

She caught at his arm.

'No! No!' she protested. 'People will be coming — they'll be wanting to know what's wrong. I mustn't be seen. I can't talk to you here.'

Mike took her arm.

'Where shall we go?'

'My flat,' she answered. 'I — I haven't dared go near it all day, but — but it will be safe if you're with me. It's not far away.'

'Let's go,' said Mike.

The block of flats was two streets away.

'We'll use the back entrance,' she said. 'I — I don't want to use the front. You'll understand after I've talked to you.'

Mike entered a narrow doorway and then followed her up a narrow staircase. He hadn't far to climb for she stopped outside a door on the first floor. As she turned the key in the lock, Mike's hand went into his jacket pocket.

The girl had been afraid to return to

her flat alone. It would be just as well if he kept his gun handy.

The light was switched on and he found himself looking into a small hall. He followed her then into a well-furnished sitting-room. Everything bore the mark of good taste, and Mike realised that the girl in red was no ordinary bird of passage.

'We'd better have a look at your injury now,' he suggested.

Tenderly she felt her head. 'It's only a scratch,' she said. 'He caught me a glancing blow. I'm a bit shaken though, and a drink is definitely indicated. I'll get you one while I'm about it.'

She crossed to a cocktail cabinet. Opening the top, she took out a decanter of whisky and a soda syphon.

'Will you take it straight?' she enquired.

'Straight, please,' said Mike.

She poured at least three fingers into each glass.

'Cheers!' she said, and drained the glass at a gulp.

'Cheers!' toasted Mike, and felt it was only good manners to do likewise. He pulled a chair forward. 'What is it you have to tell me?' he asked.

She shook her head.

'There's no hurry now,' she said. 'Not now that I'm safe in the flat. I'd like to attend to this scratch and then to clean myself up a little. I'll only be a few minutes.'

She opened a door, and before she closed it behind her, he caught a glimpse of a well-appointed bathroom. He wondered how she fitted into the mystery of the professor's disappearance. Whoever she was, she was hard-boiled.

Time went by and Mike began to feel sleepy. He tried to stretch his legs and found he could hardly move them. Suddenly, his eyes went wide, and he seized the arms of the chair. Slowly — painfully — he forced himself to his feet.

As he did so the bathroom door opened and the girl in red reappeared. She lounged in the doorway, a hand poised elegantly on her hip.

'In trouble — sucker?' she asked.

He tried to force his hand into his jacket pocket.

'What — did — you — put — in — my — drink?' he asked, and each word was an effort.

She moved towards him, her lips curled in contempt.

Coolly — deliberately — she placed a hand against his chest and forced him back into the chair. Mike collapsed and found that he could not move again.

'You've had it, sucker!' she told him. 'You fell for the old gag like a newborn babe.'

The dreadful thing was that his brain remained clear. He could think, but he could not act. What manner of drug had she given him?

Once again he had fallen down. The 'phone call could never have come from Sir Redvers — it had been someone cleverly imitating his voice. And he had had no suspicion. No wonder the girl was contemptuous! He had indeed been a prize sucker. But maybe this girl in red wasn't holding all the cards. She slapped his face, first with her left hand and then with her right. His head tilted under the impact, but that was all. The drug had made him as helpless as a log.

'You've taken it all right,' she said. 'Good stuff, don't you think? Whisky — straight! What a laugh!'

She swayed towards a telephone, lifted the receiver and dialled a number. After a while, she spoke.

'I've got the goods. Twelve stone of helpless he-man! You can collect as soon as you like!'

6

A Wedding Has Been Disarranged

Mike's brain remained clear. Time and time again he tried to move, but nothing happened. He tried to speak but the words refused to come.

What an idiot he had been! Nevertheless, the gang had planned this coup with great care. The girl had even gone to the length of making a small cut in her head. The phoney attack upon her had been to make sure that she had a real excuse to decoy him to her flat. Even the drugged glass must have already been prepared, because he was certain she had poured nothing into it except whisky.

There was a ring at the front door. The girl hurried to answer it, but closed the door of the sitting room after her. Nothing happened for a minute or two. Then the door opened and Mike was gazing at the gowned figure with the grotesque mask. At the sight of him, his mind was filled with a seething fury, but his body remained inactive.

The unknown glided forward in his noiseless manner.

'So, my friend, you surprised me yesterday,' the figure said blandly. 'I wonder just how you made your way to Greytowers. But it is not very important now. You see, this time, my friend, there will be no mistakes.'

Mike sat and stared at him and the agony of his helplessness was acute.

'I could take no risks yesterday,' the voice went on. 'For all I knew the police were at your heels. So I thought it necessary to leave and to take Professor Weston with me. It was much against the grain that I left the lovely Miss Weston with you.' He chuckled. 'You must be dying to fly at my throat,' the unknown continued. 'But your powers of move-ment will not return for some time yet. When it does, it will be too late. You have interfered with my plans, Carr, and no man does that and goes on living. Quite soon you will be taken from here and you will be carried to the river. Maybe your body will be found — maybe not. Either way, your death will remain an unsolved mystery.'

Mike willed himself to move.

'You are luckier than Miss Weston,' the cold voice went on. 'She has set her will against mine and so her determination must be broken. Tomorrow she will be in my power, and from then onwards she is destined to play the part of my slave. Understand that, Carr — *my slave!* Her soul will be mine to work to my will, and I intend that she shall suffer. You are the lucky one, Carr. Lucky to die.'

Mike could only sit and stare.

'Let this be your last thought,' said the voice. 'Lovely Jennifer will be my abject slave until she dies. You should pray that she does not live too long.'

He clapped his hands together and the girl in red swayed into the room.

'You have done well,' said the mask. 'Within a few minutes they will come to take him away. The power of the drug does not last forever, and he must be placed in the river while its power is still strong upon him. After he has gone, leave this flat and do not return again, my dear.'

The girl nodded.

The gowned figure glided to the door.

'I almost regret your inability to speak, Carr,' he crowed. 'I'm sure you'd wish me joy of the lovely Jennifer!'

The door closed and he was gone.

The girl in red sauntered over to Mike and lifted up his chin. Then she felt his arms.

'A pity you had to fall foul of the boss,' she commented. 'You and I could have gone places together.'

It was only a matter of minutes before the door opened again and two men entered. Again, Mike wanted to catapult from his chair. They were the same two men who had abducted Jennifer — the same two whom he had had the pleasure of knocking out cold.

They stood glowering down at him.

'Do we beat him up first, Jim?' demanded one.

The other clenched his hands, half started forward, and then shook his head.

'We've got to get him into the river,' he rapped. 'The boss told us to hurry — that drug might begin to wear off. If we make sure that he drowns, I reckon we can call it quits.'

'I guess so,' said the other. 'Give me a hand with him.'

They dragged Mike to his feet, and each placed an arm around him.

'Goodbye, sucker,' said the girl in red. 'I'm still sorry we couldn't go places together.'

Mike gave the impression of being the worse for liquor as they dragged him out of the apartment. Perhaps that was the scene they wanted to create. Out of the flats, they supported him, and then bundled him into the back of a waiting car. Mike's last hope deserted him. So the girl in red had held all the cards after all. The car moved away from the curb. As it turned into Farr Street, one of the men in the front raised an alarm.

'There's a car right on our tail!' he shouted. 'Step on it!'

But the other car was already travelling at speed. It drew out as though to pass. It was almost level when it suddenly swung inwards.

'Look out!' came the frantic yell.

There was a grinding of metal and Mike's car was forced on to the pavement. There was a sickening crash as it tried to wrap itself round a lamp-post, and Mike was thrown forward over the seat in front.

Out of the wreckage climbed two frightened men who took to their heels and disappeared into the darkness.

The driver of the second car came racing back. He pulled open a door of the wrecked vehicle.

'Are you all right, guv?' he demanded hoarsely. 'It was the only way, guv.'

Mike saw Slug Emery looking down at him. So the girl in red hadn't held all the cards after all. Ever since taking the drug, he had been counting on Slug.

He tried to speak and this time words came.

'Get — me — out,' he gasped. 'Get — me — home.'

'You're on your way,' said Slug. 'Take it easy, boss.'

He had Mike out of the back seat in a jiffy. He realised something was wrong, but he didn't stop to ask, knowing that Mike wouldn't want to be questioned by the police if it could be avoided. At a shambling run he half-carried him to the other car, which had escaped any serious damage.

As Slug's foot went down on the accelerator, a policeman appeared out of the gloom.

'Wait a moment!' he yelled. 'What's happened here?'

'Some other time!' said Slug. The car shot forward and the policeman jumped for safety.

When they reached the cottage Mike found that he could use his legs a little. The effects of the drug were working off.

'I carried out instructions, guv,' Slug assured him. 'I had the car at the end of Farr Street sharp on eight o'clock. I saw you go away with the girl in red and then I lost you at the back of those flats. I thought you'd gone inside, but I couldn't be sure. Then a car drew up and a guy got out. I thought there was something queer about him from the way he kept his face hidden. He used the back door of the flats. When he came out again he spoke to the men in the car and then he walked away. Two men got out of the car and they entered the flats. When they came out again you were between them, guv. I knew there was something wrong so I raced for the car. They came to meet me by turning into Farr Street and I did the first thing that came into my head — I ran 'em down.'

Slowly, still speaking with the greatest difficulty, Mike told him what had happened.

'Get me a coffee, Slug,' he said at last. 'I'm not feeling too good.'

Despite the coffee, he found he couldn't keep awake. In fact, he almost fell asleep standing up, and Slug was compelled to put him to bed. Mike slept like a log.

In the morning he was back to normal. He could talk, and all signs of stiffness had left his body. But with the morning came fear — fear for Jennifer.

Going to the 'phone, he rang Jennifer's flat. He caught his breath when he got the 'no answer' signal. Had the masked fiend struck already?

'*Slug!*' he yelled. 'Wash out breakfast. Get the car out. We're going to town. *Hurry!*'

He risked a summons for speeding every yard of the way. Reaching Windmere Mansions, he raced inside.

'Miss Weston's apartment,' he said to the liftman.

The man stared at him.

'You're unlucky, sir,' he said. 'Miss Weston left last night. She expects to be away for some months.'

Mike felt himself go cold. So he was too late. The masked fiend had already struck.

'Er — thanks,' he said and raced back to the car.

'Sir Redvers now,' he said to Slug. 'He's my only hope.'

But he knew that it was unlikely that Sir Redvers could give him any guidance. He might not even find him at his office.

Brushing by the secretary outside the

door, he dashed inside. Sir Redvers *was* at his desk.

'Hello,' the chief greeted. 'This is an early visit, Mike. I'm not usually here at this hour. But I'm so worried over this Weston case — '

'That's what I've come about,' gasped Mike. 'Miss Weston left her flat last night. I'm sure she's been kidnapped again.'

If he had expected Sir Redvers to be shocked, he was disappointed.

The chief simply smiled at him.

'Oh, no,' he said, 'I don't think Miss Weston has been kidnapped this time. At least it isn't usually called kidnapping.'

Mike stared at him — almost fearing to hope.

'You *know* where she is?' he queried. 'She — she's all right?'

Sir Redvers picked up a letter from his desk.

'This has just arrived,' he said. 'I think it explains everything. It's from Neil Rawson.'

Mike took the letter and stared at the bold, upright handwriting.

Dear Sir Redvers,

Being very concerned for Miss Weston's safety I am taking steps to be with her at all times. In other words, I am hurrying forward our marriage. Shortly after you receive this — at eleven o'clock at Holloford Registry Office — we will be made man and wife. I shall not let her out of my sight until this mystery has been cleared up. I give you this information so that you will not worry while Miss Weston is away from her flat for a few days.

Yours,

Neil Rawson.

'About the best thing that could happen,' said Sir Redvers, stealing a glance at Mike. 'With a husband to look after her — why, what's the matter, Mike?'

Mike was still staring at the letter — staring as though he could not credit the evidence of his eyes.

'Listen,' he gasped. 'I've no time to explain. But this is what you must do. Everything depends upon it.'

Mike spoke rapidly in an urgent

undertone. Sir Redvers listened and his jaw dropped a little.

'I can't go giving crazy orders like that,' he objected.

Mike made for the door.

'You must!' he insisted. 'You must make sure that the police take no action. That's all. If you don't, you'll regret it as long as you live.'

The door slammed behind him.

7

A Bride is Kidnapped

On leaving the office, Mike raced to the nearest call box and put through two long calls. As he hurried back to the car he looked surprisingly satisfied with himself.

'Slug,' he said, 'something's happened and we've a job to do. The most important part of it is to get to Holloford before eleven o'clock. This is what we do when we get there.'

He explained with care and at length. As he listened, Slug's eyes grew wider and wider.

'But — but we daren't, guv,' he gasped. 'If the crowd gets hold of us they'll tear us limb from limb. You see, a wedding's a sort of sacred affair.'

'It's going to be done,' said Mike firmly.

'Yes, guv,' Slug said meekly.

Mike arrived at Holloford with a full

quarter-of-an-hour to spare. He stationed himself some little distance from the steps leading to the registry office. For fully ten minutes he concentrated on the contents of a jeweller's window.

He saw a car drive up and out of it stepped Neil Rawson. He was dressed with care and he looked surer of himself than ever. Rawson swung open the other door. Jennifer stepped out, and it seemed to Mike that he was seeing her for the first time. She was unutterably lovely. Surely he could not have held this vision in his arms; surely it could not have been that wonderful mouth which had melted under his kisses?

Jennifer took Rawson's arm and turned her face to smile up at him. It was a smile full of trust. Seeing that smile, Mike ought to have realised that the happenings at Greytowers had meant nothing — that Jennifer was still in love — always had been in love — with Neil Rawson. But, as the two started to cross the pavement, Mike hurried forward impulsively.

'Excuse me!' he said.

Rawson turned as though he had been shot. Jennifer turned, too, and it was embarrassment that came into her eyes at the sight of Mike. But he did not look at Jennifer.

'This is for a wedding present!' he said.

His fist swung and it carried every ounce of his weight behind it. Rawson had no time to avoid the blow. He took it full on the chin and nearly dragged Jennifer with him.

An onlooker screamed.

Mike caught Jennifer when she was off-balance and swung her into his arms.

'Let me go!' she shouted. 'You brute! What the blazes do you think you're doing?'

'I'm the only man you are going to marry,' said Mike tensely.

She struck at his face. At that moment, a car glided in front of Rawson's vehicle and the near-side back door swung open. Three steps carried Mike to it. The stupefied onlookers caught a glimpse of kicking, silk-clad legs, and then Jennifer had been half-thrown, half-pushed into the car. Mike dived in after her.

'Step on it, Slug!' he rapped.

'Yes, guv,' said Slug, and his brow was damp with perspiration. 'Oh, lor'!'

The car shot forward and went round a corner on two wheels.

'Let me out!' yelled Jennifer. 'I hate you! Neil told me all about you.'

Mike discovered he had a wildcat on his hands.

'I don't like doing this, Jennifer,' he said, 'but it's just got to be done.'

He exerted his tremendous strength. Forcing her down on the seat, he gripped her wrists and held them with one hand.

'Those handcuffs, Slug,' he rapped.

'Oh, lor'!' said Slug, 'Yes, guv!'

He took a pair of handcuffs from the pigeonhole in the dashboard and handed them over the back of his seat. Mike took them and snapped them over Jennifer's wrists.

'You brute!' she gasped. 'You — you caveman, I'll — I'll — ' He stifled her scream with his handkerchief. She kicked at him so that he was forced to grab her legs and then tie her ankles together with her coloured scarf.

Slug looked as though the end of the world was near.

'We'll never get away with it, guv,' he said. 'Somebody's sure to have taken our number. The police will stop us any moment.'

'They won't,' interrupted Mike. 'Sir Redvers has given instructions to the police that all information received today concerning missing brides is to be ignored. At least, those were the instructions I gave him.'

'Oh!' said Slug, and it was a snort of relief. 'That's different.'

'So you've no need to step on it,' Mike went on. 'Just keep to a steady, easy pace.'

'Yes, guv,' said Slug doubtfully.

Mike sat back in the car and looked straight ahead. Never once did he turn to look at Jennifer. Her eyes were ablaze with hatred — and it was hatred against him. He could not bear to look.

Holloford was on the fringe of the suburbs, and so, in a very short while, Slug was driving through open country.

'The first turning on the left,' said Mike suddenly.

Slug drove underneath trees and along a rutted road that was little better than a cart-track. It led to a clearing and in the middle of it was a small house.

'Our destination,' commented Mike. 'You can pull up, Slug.'

The car glided to a stop. The house showed no signs of life.

'Give me a hand with her, Slug,' said Mike.

Jennifer's eyes still blazed hatred at him, and Mike avoided looking at her. Between them, they carried her to the house, and the door swung open as Mike pushed against it. It had been standing ajar.

'Down here,' said Mike. He led the way to a bedroom on the ground floor and indicated that Jennifer was to be placed on the bed.

'There's a shed out at the back,' he said. 'You'll find some rope there. Bring it in. It looks as though we'll have to tie her down.'

For the first time since he had known Mike, Slug looked rebellious.

'I don't like it, guv,' he protested. 'This

ain't our usual kind of business. I don't mind a spot of ordinary dirty work, but I mean — a girl — '

'It's for her own safety. Get the rope!' rapped Mike.

'Yes, guv,' said Slug.

Mike took the gag from her mouth.

'I had to keep you quiet, my dear,' he said. 'But it doesn't matter now.'

Her eyes blazed more than ever.

'I shall never forgive myself,' she said bitterly. 'I must have been *mad* when I let *you* make love to *me*. But I — I didn't know *then*. Neil told me all about you this morning — told me of all the dreadful things you've done.'

Slug came in at that moment, and Mike snapped: 'Give me the rope.'

Slug handed it over without a word and Jennifer was tied to the bed.

'Sorry to upset you, Slug,' said Mike, 'but we've got to make the future Mrs. Michael Carr see reason.'

He led the way back into the hall. Here two men were waiting, holding guns. They meant business.

'Put your hands up!' rasped one of

them. 'We're not fooling.'

The newcomers were the two men who had first abducted Jennifer, and had later been given the task of drowning Mike.

'Anything to oblige,' murmured Mike and slowly his hands went up. Slug followed suit. A voice came from the end of the hall.

'What's happening here?'

The two men with guns whirled and saw armed C.I.D. men standing in the open door.

'Take the other, Slug!' Mike shouted and flung himself at the man who had struck Jennifer. Slug was quick to follow him. Slug's victim went crashing backwards and his gun slid across the floor.

'I swore to batter your face to a pulp,' stormed Mike. 'I'll fix you so that you never strike another woman.'

For a full ten minutes the battle raged until the two crooks were crawling on the floor and whining for mercy.

Mike dragged his victim to his feet.

'I'm not through with you yet,' he snarled. 'You're going to do *exactly* as I tell you or else you'll get another bashing.'

The crook could only mumble in terror.

One of the C.I.D. men in the doorway came forward.

'What's going on, Mike?' he demanded.

'It's all in a good cause, Pete,' Mike said. 'You'll have no complaints when it's all over. But I've got to work on these two birds now. It's a matter of life or death for Miss Weston's father.'

The crooks were dragged into a sitting-room, and Mike held his victim by the front of his collar.

'You know how to get in touch with your boss, don't you?' he demanded. 'Get him on the 'phone.'

The other hesitated. But when Mike lifted his free hand, he cringed.

'Y-yes,' he faltered. 'I — I guess so.'

'Then,' said Mike. 'You're going to ring him up. This is what you're going to tell him . . . ' He explained at length.

Ten minutes later the crook dialled a number.

'Boss,' the crook said, 'we've got the

girl. Carr took her to a house in Highley Woods. It's the first turning on the left after you go right at the Highley crossroads. Yes, we had trouble with Carr. Both he and his men are down in the cellar now, and you won't have any further trouble from them. But now we're having trouble with the girl. She's in a terrible state. Shall we wait for you — ?'

A voice crackled in the receiver. Then the crook said: 'There's only Jim and me here, boss. Nobody knows anything about the rumpus.'

The unknown voice crackled again, and the crook answered: 'O.K., boss.'

He turned from the receiver.

'He's on his way,' the crook told Mike defeatedly.

'I've not finished with you,' Mike said. 'You've still got another part to play. And if you make any mistakes, I'll kill you.'

He gave further instructions and then went back to the bedroom. Jennifer turned her head and he saw the hatred still blazing in her eyes. Bending down he pulled the gag away.

'Go away!' she gasped. 'Don't come

near me. I hate you — *hate you.*'

With masterful deliberation, Mike pressed his mouth to her squirming lips.

Slug was watching wide-eyed through the doorway.

'I just don't know what's got into the guv,' he murmured. 'Sure beats me! He's usually so gentle with dames.'

8

The Brand of the Beast

A car bumped down the cart track leading to the house in the woods. At the edge of the clearing it stopped, but the driver made no move to leave his seat. For a long while he sat staring at the house. It showed no signs of life.

Suddenly the door opened. A man appeared and he looked in the direction of the car. Then he raised his hand in greeting.

The man in the car appeared to be satisfied. He engaged his clutch again and drove up to the door.

It was Neil Rawson who alighted.

He entered the house and the two crooks were there to greet him. Neil started at the sight of them.

'What the heck's happened to your ugly mugs?' he demanded.

The man who had been beaten up by

Mike lied in the way he had been forcibly instructed. 'There was a roughhouse, boss. It was some time before we got a chance to use our guns. We didn't make any mistakes then. But the girl — she's like a wildcat. We've had to lock her in a room. Here's the key.'

Neil Rawson snatched it from him.

'Where is she?' he demanded.

The other indicated the bedroom at the end of the hall. Rawson unlocked the door, stepped into the room, and closed the door behind him.

Jennifer was seated on the edge of the bed. At the sight of her visitor she came quickly to her feet, saying bitterly: 'I was hoping I'd never see you again, Neil.'

He moved nearer, pretending to be puzzled.

'What's wrong, darling?'

'I'm not drugged now,' she said angrily. 'You can't make me believe your lies any more. I know now that you've been giving me drugs for a long time. It was only because of the drugs that I agreed to marry you in the first place.'

'Jennifer!' Neil Rawson protested. 'It's

not true. Those tablets I gave you were for your headaches.'

'Keep away from me!' she screamed at him. 'In the car coming here, Mike told me all about you. When he put me into the car, I knocked my head and that seemed to free my mind of the drug. He told me then all that he had discovered about you. It was you who kidnapped my father — it is you who have been torturing him. You are the fiend who had me abducted. And — and in that horrible house — you got them to take my clothes away.' A shudder shook her. 'Down — down in that cellar, it was you who menaced me,' she accused. 'You were going to torture me. You would have done if it hadn't been for Mike.' She paused for breath. 'Well, you did me one good turn. In that cellar I learned the true meaning of love. It was Mike who taught me.'

Neil Rawson came close to her.

'What are you trying to tell me?' he asked and his voice was barely a whisper. 'Do you mean that down in the cellar, you and Mike Carr — ?'

She broke in: 'You're finished, Neil. The police know about you, and now you're a wanted man. You'll never escape the police. I shall be married to Mike. I shall be living with him while you're in prison.'

He laughed. 'I doubt it. Mike Carr's dead.'

She stared at him and caught her breath. It couldn't be true. She looked defiantly at Rawson. He was no longer handsome. His eyes were the merest slits, his mouth a hard, cruel line. Suddenly he lunged towards her. He moved so quickly that she had no chance to avoid him. He flung her back on the bed, his lithe fingers closing on her throat.

'So the police are wise to me!' he taunted. 'They know that I kidnapped your father. Even if they catch up with me, they'll never find him. He'll die a lingering death of starvation. And you — you're the only woman I ever wanted — and you gave your kisses to Carr. Now it's my turn.'

He brought his leering face near to hers. Then his whole body stiffened.

'*Rawson!*'

The voice came from behind him. He turned and saw Mike inside the room. For the moment he was stupefied. He could only stand and stare. That moment was his undoing, because Mike was already in action as Neil Rawson tried to draw his gun from his pocket.

'Get *out*, Jennifer,' he yelled.

She fled from the room. As she stumbled into the hall, Slug Emery closed the door and then took her hands in a comforting grasp.

'The guv will be all right,' he said. 'This is the way he wants it.'

Uproar came from the bedroom. Heavy bodies thudded against the walls and there was the sound of smashing furniture. It went on and on until it seemed it would never stop.

Jennifer caught Slug's shoulders.

'I can't stand it!' she moaned. 'Neil wasn't human. He was a mad brute. And — and a madman has terrible strength — '

The door opened. Something reeled across the hall to hit the far wall and then slide down into a heap. It was Neil Rawson!

Mike appeared in the doorway. His face was a mask of blood. Claw-like fingers had torn flesh from his face.

Jennifer flung herself into his arms.

★ ★ ★

A telephone call brought Sir Redvers Trevor racing to the house in the woods.

'Things have happened far too fast for me,' he said. 'I still don't understand it all.'

'Rawson made one mistake,' Mike said. 'When he took Jennifer from my cottage he left a note behind. It was a clumsy attempt to make me think she'd walked out of her own free will. If Rawson hadn't overlooked the fact that she had left a shoe behind, I might have been fooled. But I realised almost at once that the note was a forgery, and I went to great pains to memorise the handwriting.

'Then Rawson made another mistake. He sent you a letter telling you he was going to marry Jennifer. He had no fear of me then. He thought my body was in the Thames. But you showed me the note. The writing was more upright than that on the note, but many of the letters were the same. I knew then that Rawson was the man in the mask. I knew, too, that I had to save Jennifer from him even if it meant kidnapping her at the altar.'

Sir Redvers still frowned.

'But the pieces of the jigsaw still don't fit,' he objected.

'They soon will,' Mike assured him. 'Rawson had worked on part of the professor's invention, but he didn't know the whole of it. Neither did he know the code. He has told me he was offered a king's ransom for the invention. It was easy for him to kidnap Jennifer's father, but the professor kept his secret even under torture. So Rawson decided to make Jennifer reveal the code.

'He arranged for her to be taken from the restaurant. He must have seen me follow her, and then he must have followed me. It was easy for him to keep on my tail, and that's how he came to spirit Jennifer from the cottage. Then, after taking her to Greytowers, he must have come straight to you. That could have been before, or after, he threatened Jennifer. You see, she has little knowledge of the passage of time after her abduction. Rawson kept her drugged.'

'Thank goodness Jennifer left that lipstick message for you!' Sir Redvers said. 'If it hadn't been for that, we should never have grown wise to Rawson.'

Mike nodded. 'His biggest shock was when I turned up at Greytowers,' he went on. 'He was clever there. He didn't know how much we knew, so he played it safe by bringing in the police himself. I must admit, I had no suspicions of him then.'

Mike's arm went round Jennifer and he held her tight.

'I had to get tough with Jennifer today,' he confessed. 'It was the only way. You see, when I bundled her into the car, I realised there was something wrong. Her eyes were dilated and that indicated she was under the influence of drugs. I had a tough job making her normal. I wanted her to be in full possession of her senses so that she would be able to trick the truth out of Rawson. I felt that the similarity of the note and the letter wasn't sufficient proof. With Jennifer's help — knowing his desire for her — I reasoned he would condemn himself of his own mouth. And so I had to be firm with poor Jennifer until her brain was cleared of the dope.'

'He was like a primitive caveman, Sir Redvers,' Jennifer said with a laugh. 'But when my brain cleared, the relief was something I'll never forget. After Mike had bullied some sense into me, he told me exactly what he wanted me to do — and the result was that he trapped a confession out of Neil Rawson.'

Sir Redvers nodded. 'Very clever.' The chief pulled at the lobe of his ear. 'What about Professor Weston?'

Tenderly, Mike felt his scratched face.

'Rawson talked after I'd given him a spot of persuasion,' he said. 'He named all the people who were helping him, and he told me about the professor's present prison. I've already told the police, and by now the professor should have been rescued.'

Sir Redvers looked relieved.

'I talk a lot about your luck, Mike,' he said. 'But I must admit you sometimes use your brain. It was pretty quick thinking that brought Rawson to this house.'

'It seemed fairly obvious,' said Mike. 'I knew he was likely to have bodyguards on hand, and that they would be sure to follow if I abducted Jennifer. My only fear was that he would refuse to come here — that he would smell a rat. However — he came!'

That night, Mike met his future father-in-law. The professor was weak and ill, but no permanent harm had been done.

'Neil Rawson didn't disguise himself before me,' said Professor Weston. 'And that was my greatest agony — the knowledge that he intended to marry Jennifer.'

Later still, Jennifer and Mike stood in the garden. A bright moon sailed the sky. He took her in his arms.

'Darling,' he said, 'this is the start of my vacation and I don't intend to waste a single second of it.'

Her lips moved against his. 'Oh, Mike, from now onwards our lives are going to be one long holiday.'

'You mean — honeymoon,' he chuckled. 'Come over here where it's dark.'

We do hope that you have enjoyed reading this large print book.

Did you know that all of our titles are available for purchase?

We publish a wide range of high quality large print books including:
Romances, Mysteries, Classics
General Fiction
Non Fiction and Westerns

Special interest titles available in large print are:
The Little Oxford Dictionary
Music Book, Song Book
Hymn Book, Service Book

Also available from us courtesy of Oxford University Press:
Young Readers' Dictionary
(large print edition)
Young Readers' Thesaurus
(large print edition)

For further information or a free brochure, please contact us at:
Ulverscroft Large Print Books Ltd.,
The Green, Bradgate Road, Anstey,
Leicester, LE7 7FU, England.
Tel: (00 44) **0116 236 4325**
Fax: (00 44) **0116 234 0205**

THE WHISPERING WOMAN

Gerald Verner

Paula Rivers, a beautiful, haughty young cinema cashier, is selling tickets when her sister Eileen delivers a portentous note to her: *'Be careful. People who play with fire get badly burned. Sometimes they die.'* Not long afterward, Paula is found murdered in her booth, shot from behind. Who was the haggard old woman dressed in black who had accosted Eileen and told her to give Paula the note? Called to investigate, Superintendent Budd is faced with one of the most curious mysteries of his career.

MURDER FORETOLD

Denis Hughes

Agent John Bentick is not enjoying his
latest assignment for British Intelligence
— personal bodyguard to Nargan, an
abrasive foreign diplomat on a covert
mission to exchange military secrets.
On their arrival at the isolated house
of Professor Dale in Cornwall, Bentick
senses an atmosphere of mystery and
menace generated by Dale's latest invention — a sinister machine that is somehow
shaping the destiny of everyone in the
house. Soon he finds himself a helpless
pawn in a figurative chess game that
can only end in death . . .

THE OTHER MRS. WATSON'S CASEBOOK

Michael Mallory

The indomitable Amelia Watson, second wife of the famous doctor, continues to bend her formidable intellect to solving further crimes. Whether foiling anarchists, investigating a possible murder committed high above the streets of London, rescuing her old theatre colleague Harry Benbow from a decidedly awkward scrape involving a haunted house, untangling the connection behind a trail of all-too-real headless corpses, or determining the truth behind a case of apparent spontaneous combustion, this respectable Edwardian lady remains a force to be reckoned with.